Roses for the North

Performance of Shrub and Old Garden Roses at the Minnesota Landscape Arboretum

Kathy Zuzek, Marcia Richards, Steve McNamara and Harold Pellett

Minnesota Agricultural Experiment Station
University of Minnesota
Minnesota Report 237-1995

Authors: Kathy Zuzek and Steve McNamara are horticultural scientists at the University of Minnesota Horticultural Research Center. Marcia Richards is a volunteer research assistant at the Center. Harold Pellett is a professor of horticultural science at the Minnesota Landscape Arboretum. The Arboretum and the Research Center are both located in Chanhassen, Minnesota.

Acknowledgements: The authors wish to gratefully acknowledge Deborah Brown, Sam Brungardt, Bob Mugaas, and Don Selinger for their comments on this manuscript. The authors also wish to acknowledge the staff and volunteers of the Minnesota Landscape Arboretum who helped maintain and evaluate the roses for this study.

Photo editing was by Dave Hansen of the MES Educational Development System. Photography was by Dave Hansen, Kathy Zuzek, Marcia Richards, Steve McNamara and Jody Fetzer. Publication design was by Larry Etkin and John Molstad of the MES Educational Development System. Illustrations and artwork were by John Molstad and Jeff Davel. Publication manuscript editing and product management for the Minnesota Agricultural Experiment Station was by Larry Etkin.

The production of this publication was supported with funds from the Minnesota Agricultural Experiment Station. Produced in the Educational Development System, Minnesota Extension Service.

Cover: Rosa 'Applejack' Shrub Rose.

Additional copies of this publication may be available for purchase. Contact the MES Distribution Center, 20 Coffey Hall, 1420 Eckles Ave., St. Paul MN 55108-6069 for ordering information. In accordance with the Americans with Disabilities Act, this material is available in alternative formats upon request through a Minnesota county extension office, or outside of Minnesota, the MES Distribution Center (800) 876-8636.

The information in this publication is for educational purposes only. It is presented under authority granted to the Minnesota Agricultural Experiment Station, by the Hatch Act of 1887, to conduct performance trials and interpret data to the public.

Printed on recycled paper containing a minimum of 10 percent post-consumer waste. Printed with agri-based inks.

contents

'Harison's Yellow'

Introduction

Shrub Roses and Old Garden Roses are gaining in popularity across the northern tier of the United States as gardeners realize that these plants often provide excellent floral quality in combination with disease tolerance and winter hardiness. By planting these roses, gardeners can minimize pesticide use and eliminate the labor-intensive job of protecting roses from low winter temperatures.

Along with a resurgence of interest in these roses has come the realization that there is little published information comparing the growth and performance of Shrub Rose and Old Garden Rose cultivars. To provide comparative data for some of these cultivars, the Woody Ornamental Research Project at the Minnesota Landscape Arboretum conducted an evaluation program of the roses in the Arboretum's Shrub Rose Garden and research nurseries, and in a private garden near the Arboretum.

The Minnesota Landscape Arboretum is located in Chanhassen, Minnesota, a western suburb of the Minneapolis-St. Paul metropolitan area. The Shrub Rose Garden is a collection of approximately 200 hardy roses, most of which are considered Old Garden Roses or Shrub Roses. Table 1 shows the distribution of evaluated cultivars across the 23 rose classes represented.

Classes and Characteristics

Among the Old Garden Roses can be found the Gallicas, Damasks, Albas, Centifolias, and Moss Roses. These are roses that were in existence before the repeat-flowering China Rose was introduced into Europe in the late 1700s. The blending of the Old Garden Roses and the China Roses revolutionized the development of roses, giving them the ability to bloom repeatedly through a growing season. This eventually led to the development of the modern-day Hybrid Teas and Floribundas.

The Old Garden Roses differ from Hybrid Teas and Floribundas in several ways. In their growth habit, for instance, the old roses are often larger and more branched than the small, upright forms of Hybrid Teas and Floribundas.

Old Garden Roses are grown for their wide variety of mature, open flower forms, while Hybrid Tea and Floribunda flowers are considered most attractive when flower buds are only partially open. The range of flower color among the Old Garden Roses is smaller, and most cultivars within this group have only one season of bloom. This one season of bloom is often seen as a disadvantage, but in their one flush of bloom, Old Garden Roses often produce as many flowers as repeat-flowering cultivars do across their extended bloom period.

The arrangement of tightly packed petals which gives the flower a "quartered" appearance, along with a green "eye," is a common flower form among Old Garden Roses.

The Old Garden Roses are also noted for their fragrance. Among the more modern roses, fragrance is variable.

Because the Old Garden Roses are less demanding of soil conditions and have higher levels of disease resistance and winter hardiness, they are considered more carefree than Hybrid Tea and Floribunda roses.

Among the Old Garden Roses are also groups that resulted from early attempts at hybridizing the Gallicas, Damasks, Albas, Centifolias, and Moss Roses with the China Rose. These rose classes include the Chinas, Portlands, Bourbons, Hybrid Perpetuals, and Teas. Like their China Rose ancestors, these roses have glossier foliage, fewer thorns, and some potential for repeat bloom. They usually retain the floral characteristics and shrub form of their old rose ancestors.

Many other classes of roses are represented in the Minnesota Landscape Arboretum's Shrub Rose Garden. These range from the Species, or wild roses, to the few Floribundas hardy enough to survive without winter protection. Between these extremes are other classes of roses that are often collectively called "shrub roses." These resulted from the blending of the Old Garden Roses, Hybrid Teas, or Floribundas with Species Roses and their hybrids.

Some Shrub Roses will rebloom during the growing season, but it is still difficult for them to rival the rebloom of the Hybrid Teas and Floribundas. The blending of Species Rose flower form with that of the other rose classes tends to result in a mass of semi-double, informal flowers among the Shrub Rose cultivars. More often than not, Shrub Roses are larger and more branched than Hybrid Teas and Floribundas.

Performance and Evaluations

During a multi-year study, the results of which form the basis of this publication, roses were evaluated for floral traits, bloom pattern, plant size and habit, disease and insect tolerance, and winter injury. Field evaluations were conducted from 1989 through 1992. Controlled lab studies measuring mid-winter hardiness of rose canes were done over several winters between 1989 and 1994.

It should be emphasized that plant performance is always site-related. Variations in climate, soil conditions, races of pathogens and insects present, and cultural practices all affect the growth and performance of plants. The information in this publication measures performance of

Table 1. Distribution across classes of roses evaluated at the Minnesota Landscape Arboretum. There are 23 classes of roses represented.

Class	Number of Cultivars
Albas	7
Bourbons	2
Centifolias	11
Damasks	10
Floribundas	5
Gallicas	15
Grandifloras	1
Hybrid Albas	1
Hybrid Blandas	1
Hybrid Caninas	1
Hybrid Foetidas	1
Hybrid Moyesiis	2
Hybrid Musks	4
Hybrid Nitidas	2
Hybrid Perpetuals	5
Hybrid Rugosas	26
Hybrid Spinosissimas	6
Hybrid Suffultas	2
Kordesiis	10
Miscellaneous Old Garden Roses	1
Mosses	29
Shrub Roses	28
Species	26
Total	**196**

hardy roses at the Minnesota Landscape Arboretum, and should be interpreted only as an indication of how plants might perform in gardens in the Upper Midwest and Canada.

The tables in this publication list rose cultivars alphabetically within each rose class. Classification and nomenclature follow that of *Modern Roses 10.*[1]

---

[1] *Modern Roses 10,* T. Cairns, *ed.* American Rose Society, Shreveport, Louisiana. 1993.

Floral Traits

Flower form, color and size, along with inflorescence size and fragrance are highly variable traits among roses. These traits in combination have led to the infinite variation in flower appearance and fragrance found across the thousands of rose cultivars.

Flower Form

All roses were originally single, composed of five petals, with the exception of a single four-petaled species. As mutations occurred that replaced stamens and pistils with additional petals, semi-double (6 to 14 petals) and double (15 or more petals) roses appeared. These oddities were saved and propagated by gardeners. Today, a double rose is the norm, although there are also rose cultivars with single and semi-double flowers. Petal counts among rose cultivars range from five into the hundreds.

Flower form is a function of petal count and petal length. Petal length is dependent on a rose cultivar's ancestry. The petals of Old Garden Roses are typically short and numerous. The mature flower is usually very double and when fully open is flat or cupped in appearance. The arrangement of petals sometimes gives the flower a quartered appearance, and often there is a "button eye" in the flower center. Sometimes, as seen among the Centifolias, the outer petals are larger and curve up and around the short, inner petals, resulting in a mature flower with a globular form. Flower buds of Old Garden Roses are not considered very attractive.

Flowers of Hybrid Teas, Floribundas, and other rose classes with China and Tea Roses prevalent in their ancestry have a lower petal count, but their petals are larger and longer. These mature flowers have a much looser appearance than those of the Old Garden Roses. It is the partially open, high-centered buds of the Hybrid Teas and Floribundas that are considered attractive, rather than the mature flowers.

Shrub Roses, more than any other group of roses, are genetically diverse. Old Garden, China, Tea, and Species Roses are all ancestors of Shrub Roses. As a result, flower forms representative of all of these groups can be found among Shrub Rose cultivars.

Colors and Color Patterns

Pink is the predominant flower color among rose species, but there are also red, white, and yellow-flowered species. The color range among Old Garden Roses is limited to white, pink, mauve, maroon, purple, and crimson. Gallicas are the most richly colored of the Old Garden Roses, with many mauve, maroon, purple, and crimson cultivars. It is only in modern roses that yellow, orange, and true red become common.

'Rosa Mundi' is a striped or variegated form of the deep pink Gallica 'Apothecary's Rose'. The semi-double, fragrant blooms appear once each year in June.

There is also a wide variety in color pattern among roses. Some cultivars have flowers that are shaded with a subtle blending of two or more colors. Other cultivars have petals that are striped or stippled, or petals whose top and reverse are different colors. It is also common for flower color to change, intensify, or lighten as buds open and expand into mature flowers.

Flower diameter among rose cultivars varies from 1 to 6 inches. The trend in rose cultivar development has been away from smaller flower size and towards larger-flowered types, but a shrub covered with masses of small flowers can be as effective in the landscape as a larger-flowered cultivar.

Inflorescence size measures the number of blooms in a single cluster on a plant. The flowers of some cultivars are borne singly while other cultivars produce flowers in clusters of several dozen. Roses with large inflorescences have become popular as bedding plants because of their visual impact in the landscape. Of the roses grown in the Arboretum's Shrub Rose Garden, the Floribundas and Hybrid Musks are known for their large inflorescence size, while the other classes have clusters of smaller and more variable size.

Flower Fragrance

The fragrances found among rose cultivars vary both in type and intensity. Many of the Species Roses are fragrant; a few are unpleasantly scented. The Old Garden Roses and Hybrid Rugosas are typically very fragrant. During the development of modern roses, fragrance was often diminished or lost, as breeders selected for flower form and color over fragrance.

Comparison of Floral Traits

Floral traits for the cultivars and species evaluated in this study are listed in Table 2. Flower color, size, fragrance, and form were evaluated on mature flowers, using American Rose Society[2] color categories. Inflorescence size was also measured.

---

[2] *Modern Roses 10*, T. Cairns, *ed.* American Rose Society, Shreveport, Louisiana. 1993.

There are a number of texts with written descriptions and accompanying floral photographs of rose cultivars. In combination, *Roses* by Roger Phillips and Martyn Rix,[3] *Roses* by Peter Beales,[4] and *Hardy Roses* by Robert Osborne[5] cover many of the cultivars evaluated in this study.

[3] R. Philips. and M. Rix. *Roses.* Random House, Inc., New York. 1988.

[4] P. Beales. *Roses.* Henry Holt and Company, Inc., New York.1992.

[5] R. Osborne. *Hardy Roses.* Garden Way Publishing, Pownal, Vermont. 1991.

Table 2. Floral traits of the rose cultivars evaluated in the Minnesota Landscape Arboretum study. Arrangement is alphabetical by and within classes. Flower color, size, fragrance, form, and inflorescence size are measured on mature flowers. Color categories of the American Rose Society are used for that characteristic.

Color Categories:

w	=	white, near white, white blend
ly	=	light yellow
my	=	medium yellow
yb	=	yellow blend
ab	=	apricot and apricot blend
op	=	orange pink
lp	=	light pink
mp	=	medium pink
dp	=	deep pink
pb	=	pink blend
mr	=	medium red
dr	=	dark red
rb	=	red blend
m	=	mauve and mauve blend

Fragrance Ratings:

0	=	no fragrance
f	=	slight fragrance
ff	=	moderate fragrance
fff	=	strong fragrance
-f	=	unpleasant fragrance

Flower Form:

single	=	5 petals
semi	=	semi-double; 6-14 petals
double	=	15 or more petals

Flower Size:

Inches converted from centimeters are rounded to the nearest half-inch.

Cultivar	Flower Color	Flower Size (cm)	(in)	Fragrance	Flower Form	Flowers per Cluster
ALBAS						
Alba semi-plena	w	9.0	3.5	ff	semi	2-5
Belle Amour	lp	7.0	3.0	ff	semi	2-5
Chloris	lp	7.0	3.0	ff	double	2-5
Jeanne d'Arc	w	7.0	3.0	fff	double	2-5
Königin von Dänemark	lp	7.0	3.0	ff	double	2-5
Mme. Legras de St. Germain	w	5.0	2.0	f	double	2-5
Pompon Blanc Parfait	w	5.0	2.0	f	double	2-5

Cultivar	Flower Color	Flower Size (cm)	(in)	Fragrance	Flower Form	Flowers per Cluster
BOURBONS						
Gipsy Boy	m	4.0	1.5	ff	double	2-5
Mme. Ernest Calvat	lp	7.0	3.0	fff	double	2-5
CENTIFOLIAS						
Blanchefleur	w	8.0	3.0	fff	double	2-5
Bullata	mp	9.0	3.5	ff	double	2-5
Cabbage Rose	mp	7.5	3.0	ff	double	2-5
Centifolia Variegata	pb	8.0	3.0	f	double	10-15
Fantin-Latour	lp	9.0	3.5	ff	double	5-10
Petite de Hollande	mp	5.0	2.0	ff	double	2-5
Prolifera de Redouté	mp	7.0	3.0	fff	double	2-5
Red Provence	mp	7.0	3.0	ff	double	2-5
Rose de Meaux	lp	3.0	1.0	f	double	2-5
Rose des Peintres	mp	8.0	3.0	ff	double	2-5
Tour de Malakoff	dp	5.0	2.0	f	double	2-5
DAMASKS						
Autumn Damask	mp	8.0	3.0	fff	double	5-10
Césonie	dp	5.0	2.0	fff	double	5-10
Kazanlik	mp	9.0	3.5	fff	double	5-10
Léda	w	7.0	3.0	ff	double	2-5
Mme. Hardy	w	7.0	3.0	ff	double	2-5
Marie Louise	mp	7.0	3.0	ff	double	1
Omar Khayyám	mp	4.0	1.5	fff	double	2-5
Rose de Rescht	dp	7.0	3.0	ff	double	2-5
St. Nicholas	dp	8.0	3.0	f	semi	5-10
York and Lancaster	pb	8.0	3.0	ff	double	5-10
FLORIBUNDAS						
Chuckles	dp	9.5	3.5	fff	semi	10-25
Dapple Dawn	lp	9.0	3.5	f	semi	2-5
Eutin	dr	5.0	2.0	f	double	>25
Nearly Wild	mp	5.0	2.0	ff	single	15-25
Redcoat	rb	11.0	4.5	f	semi	2-5
GALLICAS						
Alain Blanchard	m	7.0	3.0	ff	semi	2-5
Alice Vena	dp	5.0	2.0	fff	double	2-5
Alika	dp	8.0	3.0	fff	semi	2-5
Belle des Jardins	m	8.0	3.0	ff	double	2-5
Belle Isis	lp	8.0	3.0	ff	double	2-5
Cardinal de Richelieu	m	7.0	3.0	f	double	2-5
Charles de Mills	dp	8.0	3.0	fff	double	2-5
Désireé Parmentier	mp	8.0	3.0	fff	double	2-5
Duchesse de Montebello	lp	7.0	3.0	fff	double	2-5
Narcisse de Salvandy	[no data — died back to the ground every year]					
Président de Sèze	pb	8.0	3.0	f	double	2-5
Rosa Mundi	pb	9.0	3.5	ff	semi	2-5
Rose du Maître d'École	mp	9.0	3.5	fff	double	2-5
Superb Tuscan	dr	7.5	3.0	f	semi	2-5
Tuscany	dr	7.0	3.0	fff	semi	1

Cultivar	Flower Color	Flower Size (cm)	(in)	Fragrance	Flower Form	Flowers per Cluster
GRANDIFLORAS						
Earth Song	dp	10.5	4.0	ff	double	2-5
HYBRID ALBAS						
Mme. Plantier	w	7.0	3.0	f	double	2-5
HYBRID BLANDAS						
Betty Bland	mp	6.0	2.5	ff	double	2-5
HYBRID CANINAS						
Andersonii	mp	7.0	3.0	ff	single	5-10
HYBRID FOETIDAS						
Harison's Yellow	my	7.0	3.0	f	semi	1
HYBRID MOYESIIS						
Marguerite Hilling	mp	13.0	5.0	f	semi	1
Nevada	w	10.0	4.0	ff	semi	1
HYBRID MUSKS						
Ballerina	pb	4.0	1.5	0	single	>25
Belinda	mp	4.0	1.5	f	semi	5-10

'Morden Centennial' is a Shrub Rose developed by Agriculture Canada in Morden, Manitoba. It is a modern, hardy Shrub Rose whose high-centered flowers appear in spring and fall. Hip production is abundant.

Cultivar	Flower Color	Flower Size (cm)	(in)	Fragrance	Flower Form	Flowers per Cluster
Daphne	w	4.0	1.5	f	semi	15-25
Will Scarlet	mr	6.0	2.5	f	semi	2-5
HYBRID NITIDAS						
Aylsham	mp	7.0	3.0	ff	double	2-5
Metis	mp	7.0	3.0	ff	double	2-5
HYBRID PERPETUALS						
Baron Girod de l'Ain	dp	8.0	3.0	fff	double	2-5
Frau Karl Druschki	w	14.0	5.5	f	double	2-5
Mme. Scipion Cochet	lp	9.0	3.5	f	double	2-5
Mrs. John Laing	mp	9.0	3.5	ff	double	2-5
Reine des Violettes	m	8.0	3.0	fff	double	2-5
HYBRID RUGOSAS						
Agnes	ly	7.0	3.0	ff	double	1
Amelia Gravereaux	dp	8.0	3.0	ff	double	5-10
Belle Poitevine	mp	8.0	3.0	ff	semi	5-10
Blanc Double de Coubert	w	9.0	3.5	ff	double	5-10
Bonavista	mp	5.0	2.0	f	double	10-15
Charles Albanel	m	8.0	3.0	ff	double	2-5
David Thompson	dp	8.5	3.5	ff	double	5-10
Delicata	pb	9.0	3.5	ff	semi	5-10
Elmira	dp	5.0	2.0	ff	double	10-15
Frau Dagmar Hartopp	lp	8.0	3.0	ff	single	2-5
George Will	dp	9.0	3.5	ff	double	2-5
Grootendorst Supreme	dp	3.0	1.0	0	double	15-25
Hansa	m	11.0	4.5	ff	double	2-5
Henry Hudson	w	6.0	2.5	ff	double	5-10
Hunter	mr	9.0	3.5	0	double	5-10
Jens Munk	mp	7.0	3.0	f	double	2-5
Martin Frobisher	lp	7.0	3.0	ff	double	2-5
Moncton	lp	5.0	2.0	f	double	2-5
Mrs. John McNabb	lp	7.0	3.0	ff	double	2-5
Pink Grootendorst	mp	3.0	1.0	0	double	15-25
Rose à Parfum de l'Hay	mp	8.0	3.0	fff	semi	2-5
Rugosa Magnifica	m	9.5	3.5	ff	double	2-5
Sir Thomas Lipton	w	8.0	3.0	ff	double	10-15
Thérèse Bauer	mp	7.0	3.0	fff	semi	5-10
Thérèse Bugnet	mp	9.0	3.5	ff	double	2-5
Will Alderman	mp	8.0	3.0	fff	double	2-5
HYBRID SPINOSISSIMAS						
Frühlingsanfang	ly	10.0	4.0	f	single	1
Frühlingsduft	yb	8.0	3.0	fff	double	2-5
Frühlingsgold	ly	10.0	4.0	f	semi	2-5
Karl Förster	w	8.0	3.0	f	double	1
Suzanne	lp	3.0	1.0	f	double	2-5
Wildenfelsgelb	ly	10.0	4.0	ff	single	1

Cultivar	Flower Color	Flower Size (cm)	(in)	Fragrance	Flower Form	Flowers per Cluster
HYBRID SUFFULTAS						
Assiniboine	mr	8.0	3.0	f	semi	2-5
Cuthbert Grant	dr	9.0	3.5	f	double	2-5
KORDESIIS						
Alexander von Humboldt	mr	8.0	3.0	f	semi	2-5
Dortmund	mr	9.0	3.5	0	single	10-15
Henry Kelsey	mr	7.0	3.0	ff	double	5-10
Illusion	mr	9.0	3.5	f	double	5-10
John Cabot	dp	8.0	3.0	ff	double	2-5
John Davis	lp	9.0	3.5	0	double	5-10
Karlsruhe	mp	10.0	4.0	ff	double	5-10
Parkdirektor Riggers	dr	7.5	3.0	0	semi	2-5
Rote Max Graf	[no data — died back to the ground every year]					
William Baffin	dp	7.0	3.0	f	double	15-25
MISCELLANEOUS OLD GARDEN ROSES						
Juno	lp	10.0	4.0	ff	double	5-10
MOSSES						
Black Boy	dr	8.0	3.0	ff	double	2-5
Capitaine John Ingram	m	4.0	1.5	f	double	2-5
Chevreul	lp	7.0	3.0	fff	double	2-5
Communis	pb	7.0	3.0	ff	double	2-5
Comtesse de Murinais	w	7.0	3.0	fff	double	2-5
Deuil de Paul Fontaine	dr	8.0	3.0	ff	double	2-5
Duchess de Verneuil	mp	7.0	3.0	fff	double	2-5
Gabriel Noyelle	ab	9.0	3.5	ff	double	2-5
Général Kléber	pb	8.0	3.0	ff	double	5-10
Gloire des Mousseuses	pb	9.0	3.5	fff	double	1
Goethe	dp	5.0	2.0	0	single	5-10
Gracilis	mp	7.0	3.0	fff	semi	2-5
Henri Martin	dp	8.0	3.0	fff	semi	5-10
Jeanne de Montfort	mp	9.0	3.5	fff	semi	5-10
Julie de Mersan	mp	8.0	3.0	ff	double	2-5
Laneii	mp	7.0	3.0	fff	double	2-5
Louis Gimard	pb	6.0	2.5	fff	double	2-5
Mme. de la Rôche-Lambert	mp	8.0	3.0	ff	double	5-10
Mme. Louis Lévêque	lp	10.0	4.0	ff	double	2-5
Mossman	lp	7.0	3.0	ff	double	2-5
Nuits de Young	dp	5.0	2.0	f	double	2-5
OEillet Panacheé	pb	7.0	3.0	fff	double	2-5
Perpetual White Moss	w	8.0	3.0	fff	double	2-5
Robert Léopold	mp	8.0	3.0	fff	double	2-5
Salet	mp	8.0	3.0	fff	double	2-5
Violacée	m	6.0	2.5	fff	double	2-5
Waldtraut Nielsen	mp	8.0	3.0	ff	double	2-5
White Bath	w	6.0	2.5	ff	double	2-5
William Lobb	m	8.0	3.0	fff	semi	5-10

Cultivar	Flower Color	Flower Size (cm)	(in)	Fragrance	Flower Form	Flowers per Cluster
SHRUB ROSES						
A. MacKenzie	rb	6.0	2.5	ff	double	5-10
Adelaide Hoodless	mr	6.0	2.5	f	semi	5-10
Alchymist	ab	9.0	3.5	f	double	5-10
Amiga Mia	lp	11.5	4.5	f	double	2-5
Applejack	mp	9.0	3.5	ff	semi	10-15
Blue Boy	dp	8.0	3.0	-f	double	1
Bonica	lp	7.0	3.0	ff	double	10-15
Carefree Beauty	mp	12.0	4.5	ff	double	2-5
Chamcook	mp	7.0	3.0	fff	double	2-5
Champlain	mr	5.5	2.0	f	double	5-10
Country Dancer	mp	11.0	4.5	f	double	2-5
Golden Wings	ly	10.0	4.0	ff	single	2-5
Haidee	lp	7.0	3.0	ff	double	1
J. P. Connell	ly	7.0	3.0	f	double	2-5
John Franklin	mr	8.0	3.0	ff	double	2-5
Lillian Gibson	mp	7.5	3.0	ff	double	15-25
Morden Amorette	mr	7.0	3.0	0	double	5-10
Morden Cardinette	rb	6.0	2.5	0	double	5-10
Morden Centennial	mp	9.0	3.5	ff	double	5-10

Rosa 'Alba semi-plena' has luminescent white, semi-double flowers with bright yellow stamens and green styles. It is one of the hardiest Albas at the Minnesota Landscape Arboretum. It blooms once in spring. It also has a spectacular hip display in the fall.

R. foetida bicolor, *commonly called 'Austrian Copper', is a Species rose. The orange petals have a yellow reverse. This rose is very susceptible to black-spot. Without fungicide protection it is a very short-lived rose at the Minnesota Landscape Arboretum.*

Cultivar	Flower Color	Flower Size (cm)	(in)	Fragrance	Flower Form	Flowers per Cluster
Morden Ruby	rb	7.0	3.0	f	double	5-10
Prairie Dawn	mp	8.0	3.0	ff	double	2-5
Prairie Princess	mp	10.5	4.0	ff	semi	2-5
Prairie Wren	lp	9.0	3.5	ff	semi	1
Prairie Youth	mp	7.0	3.0	f	semi	5-10
Robusta	mr	9.5	3.5	0	single	5-10
Scharlachglut	mr	10.0	4.0	f	single	5-10
Summer Wind	op	10.0	4.0	f	semi	5-10
Von Scharnhorst	ly	9.0	3.5	f	semi	2-5
SPECIES						
Dr. Merkeley	dp	7.0	3.0	0	double	5-10
R. amblyotis	mp	5.0	2.0	f	single	2-5
R. arkansana	mp	6.0	2.5	ff	single	10-15
R. canina	lp	4.0	1.5	f	single	5-10
R. cinnamomea	mp	5.0	2.0	ff	single	5-10
R. foetida	my	4.5	2.0	-f	single	1
R. foetida bicolor	yb	8.0	3.0	-f	single	2-5
R. glauca	mp	3.5	1.5	f	single	2-5
R. hugonis	my	7.0	3.0	f	single	1
R. laxa	w	7.0	3.0	-f	single	1
R. macounii	mp	4.0	1.5	f	single	2-5
R. mollis	mp	5.0	2.0	0	single	2-5
R. multiflora	w	3.0	1.0	0	single	2-5
R. nitida	mp	5.5	2.0	f	single	2-5
R. palustris	mp	7.0	3.0	ff	single	2-5
R. pendulina	dp	5.0	2.0	f	single	2-5
R. pomifera	mp	4.0	1.5	0	single	2-5
R. primula	my	7.0	3.0	f	single	1
R. rugosa	dp	6.0	2.5	fff	single	2-5
R. rugosa alba plena	w	9.0	3.5	fff	double	2-5
R. rugosa kamtchatica	mp	7.0	3.0	f	single	2-5
R. sertata	mp	5.5	2.0	ff	single	2-5
R. setigera	dp	7.0	3.0	f	single	15-25
R. spinosissima altaica	ly	4.0	1.5	0	single	2-5
R. virginiana	mp	5.0	2.0	fff	single	2-5
R. woodsii	mp	4.0	1.5	ff	single	2-5

Bloom Pattern

Bloom pattern describes the flowering of a rose across the growing season. Differences in bloom pattern among the hardy roses at the Minnesota Landscape Arboretum can be seen between classes as well as between cultivars within a particular class.

Most Species Roses and Old Garden Roses are one-time bloomers in Minnesota, blooming heavily in June on canes produced during previous years. Some of the Old Garden Rose classes, such as the Albas, Centifolias, and Gallicas, are genetically incapable of rebloom. Other classes, such as the Bourbons, Damasks, and Mosses, include some cultivars that have the potential to bloom a second time in late summer or early fall. Rebloom among these classes is inconsistent from year to year at the Minnesota Landscape Arboretum because of the short growing season. 'Salet', a Moss Rose, is the one exception among the Old Garden Roses, blooming lightly but reliably through summer and fall at the Arboretum.

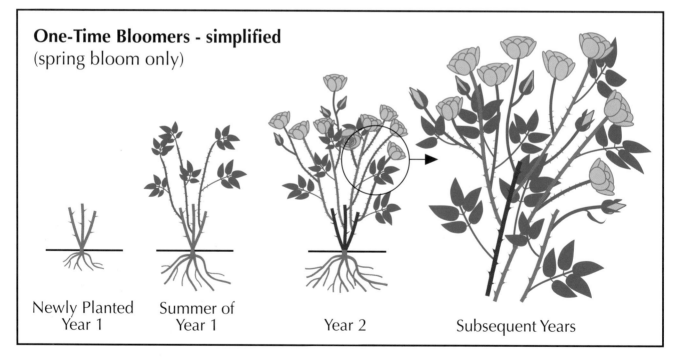

One-Time Bloomers - simplified
(spring bloom only)

Newly Planted Year 1   Summer of Year 1   Year 2   Subsequent Years

One-Time Bloomers

These plants rarely bloom in the year of planting. Beginning in year two, a pattern is established where blooms develop on the tips of previous years' wood as well as on new laterals formed on previous years' wood.

Key: green = current year's growth; light brown = one-year-old wood; dark brown = two-year or older wood.

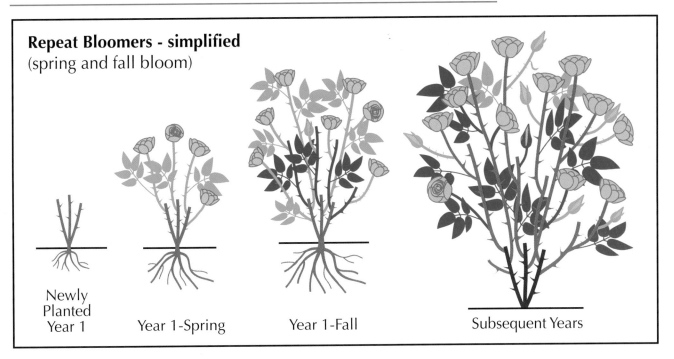

Repeat Bloomers - simplified
(spring and fall bloom)

Newly
Planted
Year 1

Year 1-Spring

Year 1-Fall

Subsequent Years

Repeat Bloomers

In the summer they are planted, repeat bloomers produce canes that bloom on the tips. New basal canes grow and may bloom at the tips in the first autumn. Additional fall flowers can be produced on laterals formed on the spring canes. During subsequent years, spring flowers are produced at the tips of new canes and on laterals formed on previous years' wood. Fall flowers may be produced at the tips of new summer canes and on laterals formed on spring canes or previous years' wood.

Key: light green = new growth in the current season; dark green = oldest growth in the current season; light brown = one-year-old wood; dark brown = two-year or older wood.

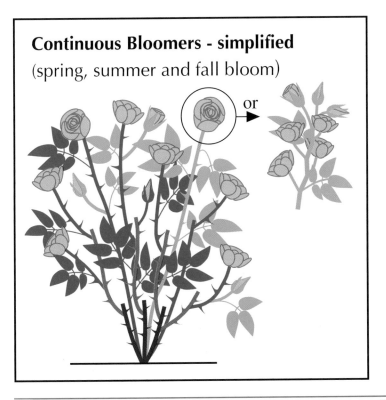

Continuous Bloomers - simplified
(spring, summer and fall bloom)

or

Continuous Bloomers

Roses which are continuous bloomers can bloom on cane tips, laterals, or from multi-branched panicles at ends of canes as soon as canes form. There are repeated cycles of cane production followed by flowering through the growing season.

Key: light green = new growth in current season; dark green = oldest growth in current season; light brown = one-year-old wood; dark brown = wood two years old or older.

Among the modern roses, some classes include both one-time bloomers and repeat bloomers. There are also classes where all of the representatives found in the Arboretum's garden have some kind of repeat bloom.

Simplifying rebloom patterns of hardy roses into a few single-word descriptions such as "repeat" and "continuous" can be confusing. The value of rebloom depends on the length of the rebloom period and on floral density, which is the number of blooms on a plant at any one time.

Heavy spring bloom is typical of most hardy roses, but flowering during summer and fall is highly variable among the cultivars. At one

Table 3. Seasonal rebloom pattern for repeat-flowering species and cultivars.

Cultivar	June Bloom	July Rebloom	August/September Rebloom
FLORIBUNDAS			
Chuckles	heavy	heavy	heavy
Dapple Dawn	heavy	moderate	heavy
Eutin	heavy	moderate	heavy
Nearly Wild	heavy	heavy	heavy
Redcoat	heavy	moderate	heavy
GRANDIFLORAS			
Earth Song	heavy	moderate	heavy
HYBRID MOYESIIS			
Marguerite Hilling	heavy	none	slight
Nevada	heavy	none	slight
HYBRID MUSKS			
Ballerina	heavy	heavy	heavy
Belinda	heavy	slight	moderate
Daphne	heavy	slight	moderate
Will Scarlet	heavy	slight	moderate
HYBRID PERPETUALS			
Baron Girod de l'Ain	heavy	none	slight
Frau Karl Druschki	heavy	none	moderate
Mme. Scipion Cochet	heavy	slight	slight
Mrs. John Laing	heavy	slight	slight
Reine des Violettes	heavy	none	slight
HYBRID RUGOSAS			
Amelia Gravereaux	heavy	moderate	moderate
Belle Poitevine	heavy	slight	slight

Cultivar	June Bloom	July Rebloom	August/September Rebloom
Blanc Double de Coubert	heavy	moderate	moderate
Bonavista	heavy	moderate	moderate
Charles Albanel	heavy	moderate	moderate
David Thompson	heavy	slight	moderate
Delicata	heavy	moderate	moderate
Elmira	heavy	moderate	moderate
Frau Dagmar Hartopp	heavy	moderate	moderate
George Will	heavy	slight	moderate
Grootendorst Supreme	heavy	moderate	moderate
Hansa	heavy	moderate	moderate
Henry Hudson	heavy	moderate	moderate
Hunter	heavy	moderate	moderate
Jens Munk	heavy	slight	moderate
Martin Frobisher	heavy	slight	moderate
Moncton	heavy	moderate	moderate
Pink Grootendorst	heavy	moderate	moderate
Rose à Parfum de l'Hay	heavy	slight	slight
Rugosa Magnifica	heavy	moderate	moderate
Sir Thomas Lipton	heavy	moderate	moderate
Thérèse Bauer	heavy	moderate	moderate
Thérèse Bugnet	heavy	slight	slight
Will Alderman	heavy	moderate	moderate
HYBRID SPINOSISSIMAS			
Karl Förster	heavy	slight	slight
Suzanne	heavy	slight	slight
Wildenfelsgelb	heavy	slight	slight
HYBRID SUFFULTAS			
Cuthbert Grant	heavy	moderate	moderate
KORDESIIS			
Alexander von Humboldt	heavy	slight	moderate
Dortmund	heavy	slight	moderate
Henry Kelsey	heavy	slight	moderate
Illusion	heavy	slight	moderate
John Cabot	heavy	moderate	heavy
John Davis	heavy	moderate	moderate
Karlsruhe	heavy	moderate	moderate
Parkdirektor Riggers	heavy	moderate	moderate
William Baffin	heavy	slight	moderate
MOSSES			
Salet	heavy	light	light
SHRUB ROSES			
A. MacKenzie	moderate	slight	slight
Adelaide Hoodless	heavy	slight	moderate
Amiga Mia	heavy	moderate	heavy
Applejack	heavy	slight	moderate
Bonica	heavy	moderate	heavy

Cultivar	June Bloom	July Rebloom	August/September Rebloom
Carefree Beauty	heavy	moderate	moderate
Champlain	heavy	moderate	moderate
Country Dancer	heavy	moderate	heavy
Golden Wings	moderate	moderate	moderate
John Franklin	heavy	moderate	moderate
J. P. Connell	moderate	none	slight
Morden Amorette	heavy	slight	moderate
Morden Cardinette	moderate	moderate	moderate
Morden Centennial	heavy	none	heavy
Morden Ruby	heavy	moderate	moderate
Prairie Dawn	heavy	slight	moderate

extreme are cultivars like 'Marguerite Hilling' and 'Nevada', commonly listed in literature as "repeat-flowering" roses. At the Minnesota Landscape Arboretum, they bloom heavily in spring, stop flowering in summer, and produce a few blooms again in fall. At the other extreme are cultivars like 'Chuckles', 'Nearly Wild', and 'Ballerina', which bloom

'Jens Munk', one of the Explorer Series roses developed by Agriculture Canada at Ottawa, Ontario, is a large, hardy rose with minimal dieback. Its R. rugosa *background gives it a wonderful combination of hardiness, disease tolerance, rebloom and fragrance.*

The Floribunda 'Nearly Wild' produces medium pink, moderately fragrant, 2-inch, single flowers. It experiences significant winter dieback, but can regrow vigorously and bloom profusely throughout the growing season.

heavily throughout spring, summer, and fall. From a flowering standpoint, these three cultivars are much more valuable as landscape plants.

The rebloom patterns for repeat-flowering cultivars and species are described in Table 3. The bloom season is divided into three periods (June, July, and August/September). Each cultivar's floral density is recorded as none, slight, moderate, or heavy for each of the three periods of the bloom season.

Cultivar	June Bloom	July Rebloom	August/September Rebloom
Prairie Princess	heavy	moderate	heavy
Prairie Youth	heavy	slight	slight
Robusta	heavy	slight	moderate
Summer Wind	heavy	moderate	moderate
SPECIES			
R. rugosa	heavy	slight	slight
R. rugosa alba plena	heavy	slight	slight
R. rugosa kamtchatica	heavy	slight	slight

Cold Hardiness

The Minnesota Landscape Arboretum is located in USDA Hardiness Zone 4a,[6] where minimum winter temperatures are commonly between –25° and –30° F (–32° to –34° C). Most rose cultivars lack sufficient cold hardiness to survive these low temperatures.

The roses in the Arboretum's Shrub Rose Garden are not given any winter protection except for a wood chip mulch that is replenished to a 4- to 6-inch depth each year. When present, snowcover provides additional winter protection, insulating canes beneath the snowline and buffering soil temperatures. But the main factor affecting plant survival is a cultivar's inherited ability to withstand harsh winter conditions.

What Cold Hardiness Is

A plant's cold hardiness has three components: acclimation, midwinter hardiness, and deacclimation. The acclimation process is triggered late in the growing season by decreasing photoperiods as daylengths shorten, and as temperatures decline. These environmental cues induce physiological and biochemical changes in the plant that result in greater cold tolerance.

Mid-winter hardiness is the lowest temperature a plant can survive without injury after it has gone through the acclimation process and has reached its maximum hardiness level.

Deacclimation refers to a decrease in the hardiness of plant tissues in response to warming temperatures in late winter and early spring.

Mid-winter hardiness levels and the rates at which acclimation and deacclimation occur for a particular cultivar or species can vary from year to year. These annual differences are caused by changes in plant health and by annual variations in temperature patterns.

The suitability of a cultivar for a particular climate depends not only on its maximum mid-winter hardiness level, but also on the timing and

---

[6] A hardiness zone map covering the United States and much of Canada is included on page 76, in the "Cultivation Tips" chapter.

rates of acclimation and deacclimation in response to environmental cues. A plant that acclimates too slowly can be injured by low temperatures in early winter. The timing and rate of acclimation have been found to be the limiting factors for the winter survivability of seven rose cultivars in Minnesota during previous research.[7]

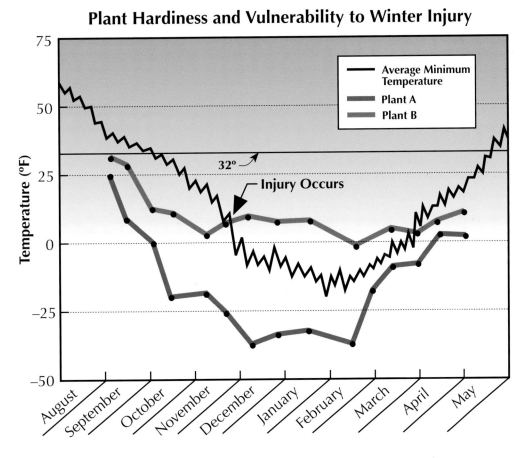

Plant Hardiness and Vulnerability to Winter Injury

When a plant's winter hardiness ratings are below the minimum temperatures which can be expected for a location, the plant's canes will not be injured (Plant A). When hardiness ratings intersect the minimum temperature line, cane injury occurs (Plant B).[8]

Plants can also be injured when mid-winter temperatures drop below a plant's maximum hardiness level. Rapid deacclimation in response to warm temperatures in late winter will also leave plants vulnerable to injury by subsequent freezing conditions.

Observations of Injury

Field observations on winter injury were conducted at the Minnesota Landscape Arboretum during early spring of 1989, 1990, and 1991.

[7] L.A. Minsk. 1993. *Acclimation of Selected* Rosa *Taxa.* Unpublished Thesis. University of Minnesota, St. Paul. 1993.

[8] Adapted from Minsk, *Acclimation of Selected* Rosa *Taxa.*

A variety of winter injury patterns were seen among the roses. Some species and cultivars exhibit no injury at all. Others show "tip" injury, where a small amount of dieback occurs at the ends of canes.

Snow serves as a natural insulator of plants, and many rose cultivars die back to the snowline. Those parts of the canes exposed to the cold air above the snow die, while the lower parts of canes covered with snow survive.

There are also cultivars that show variation in injury pattern from cane to cane. Within one plant, canes with no winter injury can be found next to canes that are either partially or completely killed.

Other cultivars behave much like herbaceous perennials, dying back to the ground every winter.

Winter injury observations for the winters of 1988-89, 1989-90, and 1990-91 are listed in Table 4. The extent of cane injury observed on the roses was categorized as none, tip, snow, <1/2 (less than half), >1/2 (greater than half), or base.

Definitions and descriptions of winter injury

None:
No injury is seen on these plants. Canes are hardy to the tip.

Tip:
Indicates injury to cane tips that resulted in dieback of 10 percent or less of the plant.

Definitions and descriptions of winter injury

Snow:
Indicates dieback
of all canes to the
snowline. Cane
material below
the snowline
remained alive.

>1/2
   (greater than half):
<1/2
   (less than half):
Mixed injury to canes;
respectively indicating
dieback of 50 percent or
less of the plant, or over
50 percent of the plant.
Cane injury within a
single plant can vary
from none to complete
kill to the ground.
Closeup of dieback in
the lower panel shows
this variable injury
pattern.

Base:
Every cane is killed
to the ground. In
spring, new canes
grow from plant's
crown.

Effects of Snowcover

The importance of snowcover as insulation is demonstrated by comparing winter injury observations for the winter of 1989-90 to those of 1988-89 and 1990-91. The minimum air temperatures at the Arboretum and average snowcover[9] on a weekly basis for the winters during which injury was recorded can be seen in the figures on page 27. Snowcover was minimal or absent during 1989-90. Many of the cultivars which typically exhibit the "snowline" pattern of hardiness died back to the ground in the absence of snowcover during that winter.

This pattern of dieback to the ground was very common among the Old Garden Roses in the winter of 1989-90. Because these roses bloom on previous years' wood, there was no bloom during spring of 1990. Cultivars of other rose classes (Floribundas, Hybrid Musks, Hybrid Perpetuals, Hybrid Rugosas, Hybrid Suffultas, Kordesiis) also died to the ground. Because these plants bloom on current year's canes as well as on previous years' wood, their flowering was less affected during the spring of 1990.

Winter Injury During Acclimation

A reduced level or a complete absence of winter injury was also observed on roses after the winter of 1988-89, in comparison to the injury sustained during the following two winters. This was seen on many cultivars among the Old Garden Roses (Albas, Bourbons, Centifolias, Gallicas, Hybrid Perpetuals, Mosses) as well as some of the Hybrid Caninas, Hybrid Moyesiis, Hybrid Spinosissimas, and Kordesiis.

If differences in minimum winter temperatures are the only comparisons made to explain annual differences in injury levels, the reduced injury level after the winter of 1988-89 seems unusual. The smallest amount of injury was observed after the coldest winter (–28° F, –33° C), while more severe injury was observed after the warmer winters of 1989-90 (–26° F, –32° C) and 1990-91 (–24° F, –31° C).

Temperature comparisons of late fall and early winter over the three years offer a more feasible explanation for the differences in winter injury patterns. Temperature declines were very gradual during late 1988. The low temperature for that winter did not occur until February 3, 1989 and the lowest temperature prior to that was –18° F (–28° C) on January 9 (top figure, page 27). This gradual temperature decline may have allowed plants to escape injury during the acclimation phase.

[9] *Climatological Data, Minnesota.* National Oceanic and Atmospheric Administration, Environmental Data and Information Service, National Climate Center. Asheville, North Carolina.

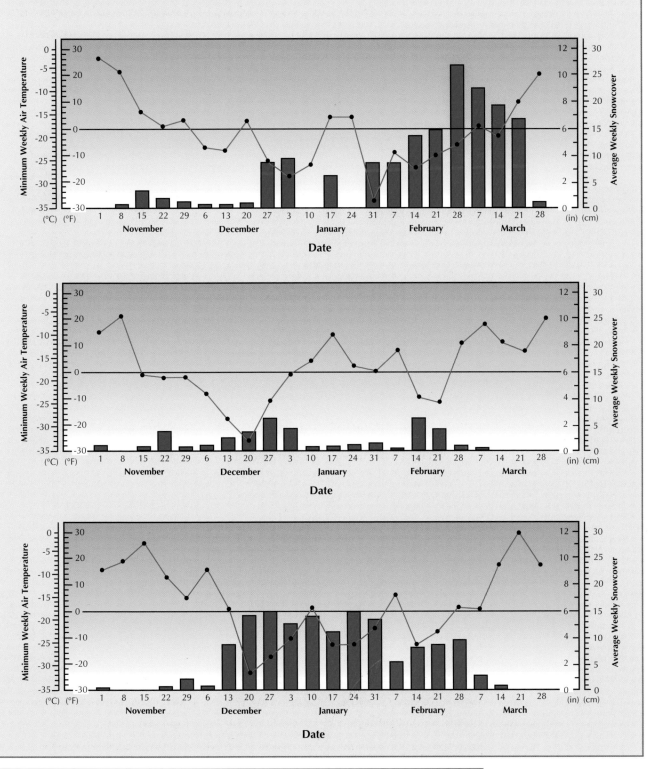

Minimum air temperatures (line graph) at the Minnesota Landscape Arboretum and the average snowcover (bar graph) on a weekly basis, for the winters during which injury was recorded—1988-89 (top), 1989-90 (middle), and 1990-91 (bottom).

Quantifying Winter Hardiness in the Laboratory

Attempts were made as part of this research to quantify mid-winter hardiness levels for 85 hardy rose cultivars and species using an ultralow-temperature freezer in a laboratory.

Cane samples from the current year's growth were harvested, placed in plastic bags, and held outdoors at ambient temperature until processed. Because of the insulating property of snow, only canes above the snowline were sampled. All the sampling occurred between January 11 and February 4 during 1990, 1991, 1993, or 1994.

Laboratory processing involved cutting the harvested canes into 1½-inch (4 cm) lengths after discarding the terminal 4 inches (10 cm) of the shoot. Ten polyethylene bags were prepared containing four cuttings each of 10 to 12 cultivars in contact with moist paper towels, which promoted ice formation at freezing temperatures.

A copper-constantan thermocouple was inserted into the center of one stem section in each bag to monitor stem temperature. The bags were closed and placed in the ultralow-temperature freezer. During this processing, no cane material was exposed to room temperature for longer than five minutes.

The samples were held overnight in the freezer at a temperature approximating the previous night's outdoor minimum temperature. An eleventh bag of cuttings was held overnight under refrigeration at 36° F (2° C) and served as a control.

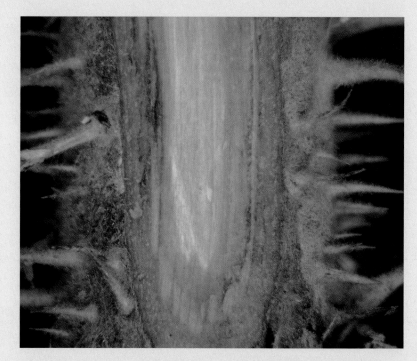

Cane section shows discoloration caused by freezing injury.

The following day, the temperature in the freezer was dropped at a rate of 10° F (5.5° C) per hour. This temperature drop was monitored through the thermocouples, which connected samples in the freezer to temperature-recording equipment outside the freezer. A temperature range was selected to bracket the estimated temperature at which cane injury would occur. As the temperature in the freezer dropped through this selected range, one bag was removed at 3° or 5° F (2° or 3°C) intervals.

The samples removed from the freezer were thawed in a refrigerator at 36° F (2° C) for 24 hours, followed by incubation at room temperature (72 ± 4° F; 22 ± 2° C) for 7 to 10 days. Stem sections were then cut lengthwise and evaluated visually for injury using a dissecting microscope. Brown discoloration of the xylem or cambium was considered fatal (see photo). The lowest sampling temperature at which 50 percent of the stem sections were uninjured was interpreted as the mid-winter hardiness level for each cultivar or species.

In contrast, the next two years had faster, more severe temperature declines during late fall and early winter (bottom two figures, page 27). The minimum temperatures during the winters of 1989-90 and 1990-91 occurred in mid- to late December rather than in early February. The higher levels of injury observed for these two years may have occurred because plants acclimated too slowly for the rapid temperature declines in early winter. When early temperature declines outpaced increases in plant hardiness, canes were injured.

Hardiness Determinations in Containers

Mid-winter hardiness determinations are made on cane tissue above the snowline on field-grown plants. However, many of the roses in the Arboretum's Shrub Rose Garden die back to the snowline by mid-winter each year, making mid-winter hardiness determinations of these plants impossible.

To circumvent the cane dieback problem, container-grown plants of some of these cultivars were placed in an overwintering greenhouse. The air temperature in the house was regulated so that roses could reach their mid-winter hardiness levels without being exposed to temperatures normally lethal to canes.

The container-grown roses were moved into the greenhouse during the first week of November after hardening under natural outdoor condi-tions. Inside the greenhouse, containers were completely covered with wood chips to a depth of 4 inches (10 cm) above the top rim to prevent cold injury to roots. The greenhouse was covered with an inflated double layer of white polyethylene. Interior air temperature was regulated with thermostatically controlled electric heaters and ventilation fans. The greenhouse was ventilated during the day to keep the temperatures inside similar to outdoor air temperatures. Minimum nighttime tempera-tures were maintained at or above 20° F (–6° C) from November 5 through December 14, and at or above –4° F (–20° C) for the remainder of the winter. Mid-winter hardiness levels were then measured in January and February using the ultralow freezer in the laboratory.

Mid-winter hardiness levels, when determined, are listed in Table 4, along with the year that cultivars or species were sampled. Table 5 lists winter injury observations from the winter of 1992-93 along with 1993 determinations of mid-winter hardiness levels for recently planted Spe-cies Roses that were not included in the main evaluation study.

Table 4. Winter injury observations and mid-winter hardiness ratings for rose cultivars, 1988–91.

Hardiness Rating: The hardiness rating is the lowest temperature at which 50 percent of the stem sections were un-injured. A "+" following a hardiness rating indicates that canes were uninjured at the lowest test temperature. The designation "(G)" next to the year indicates that cold hardiness determinations for that cultivar that year were taken from container-grown plants in an overwintering greenhouse. The designation "(I)" under the Fahrenheit and Celsius columns indicates that the canes were injured in the field prior to collection. A "—" under a winter injury column indicates that data for that variety was not recorded for that year.

| CULTIVAR | WINTER INJURY | | | MID-WINTER HARDINESS RATING | | YEAR |
	1988-89	1989-90	1990-91	Fahrenheit	Celsius	
ALBAS						
Alba semi-plena	none	tip	<1/2	(I)	(I)	1994
Belle Amour	snow	base	snow			
Chloris	none	<1/2	<1/2			
Jeanne d'Arc	none	>1/2	snow			
Königin von Dänemark	<1/2	base	snow			
Mme. Legras de St. Germain	—	>1/2	snow	−32	−36	1991 (G)
				(I)	(I)	1991
Pompon Blanc Parfait	<1/2	<1/2	snow			
BOURBONS						
Gipsy Boy	none	tip	snow			
Mme. Ernest Calvat	none	>1/2	snow			
CENTIFOLIAS						
Blanchefleur	none	>1/2	<1/2			
Bullata	none	base	snow			
Cabbage Rose	—	<1/2	<1/2			
Centifolia Variegata	none	>1/2	snow			
Fantin-Latour	<1/2	base	snow			
Petite de Hollande	none	base	snow			
Prolifera de Redouté	<1/2	>1/2	snow			
Red Provence	snow	>1/2	snow			
Rose de Meaux	snow	base	dead			
Rose des Peintres	none	base	snow			
Tour de Malakoff	<1/2	base	snow			
DAMASKS						
Autumn Damask	>1/2	base	snow			
Césonie	<1/2	<1/2	snow			
Kazanlik	snow	base	snow			
Léda	snow	>1/2	snow	−26	−32	1990 (G)
				−30	−34	1991 (G)
				(I)	(I)	1991
Mme. Hardy	none	base	>1/2	−32	−36	1991 (G)
				(I)	(I)	1991
Marie Louise	<1/2	<1/2	snow			
Omar Khayyám	<1/2	>1/2	snow			

CULTIVAR	WINTER INJURY			MID-WINTER HARDINESS RATING		YEAR
	1988-89	1989-90	1990-91	Fahrenheit	Celsius	
Rose de Rescht	snow	base	snow	−24	−31	1990 (G)
St. Nicholas	snow	>1/2	snow			
York and Lancaster	snow	>1/2	snow			
FLORIBUNDAS						
Chuckles	<1/2	base	snow			
Dapple Dawn	—	—	base			
Eutin	—	—	base	(I)	(I)	1994
Nearly Wild	snow	base	snow	(I)	(I)	1991
				(I)	(I)	1994
Redcoat	—	—	base			
GALLICAS						
Alain Blanchard	tip	base	snow			
Alice Vena	snow	>1/2	snow			
Alika	none	tip	none			
Belle des Jardins	snow	tip	<1/2			
Belle Isis	snow	>1/2	snow			
Cardinal de Richelieu	none	>1/2	snow			
Charles de Mills	none	base	snow			
Désireé Parmentier	<1/2	<1/2	snow			
Duchesse de Montebello	none	—	—	−28	−33	1990 (G)
Narcisse de Salvandy	none	base	snow			
Président de Sèze	none	>1/2	snow			
Rosa Mundi	none	>1/2	snow			
Rose du Maître d'École	none	base	snow			
Superb Tuscan	none	base	snow			
Tuscany	<1/2	base	base			
GRANDIFLORAS						
Earth Song	—	—	base			
HYBRID ALBAS						
Mme. Plantier	none	base	tip			
HYBRID BLANDAS						
Betty Bland	none	tip	tip	−36	−38	1991
HYBRID CANINAS						
Andersonii	tip	>1/2	snow	(I)	(I)	1991
HYBRID FOETIDAS						
Harison's Yellow	none	none	none	−38	−39	1991
HYBRID MOYESIIS						
Marguerite Hilling	tip	>1/2	snow	(I)	(I)	1991
Nevada	tip	>1/2	snow	(I)	(I)	1991
HYBRID MUSKS						
Ballerina	—	—	base			
Belinda	base	base	snow			

CULTIVAR	WINTER INJURY			MID-WINTER HARDINESS RATING		YEAR
	1988-89	1989-90	1990-91	Fahrenheit	Celsius	
Daphne	snow	base	snow			
Will Scarlet	<1/2	base	snow			
HYBRID NITIDAS						
Aylsham	<1/2	tip	tip			
Metis	tip	<1/2	tip	(I)	(I)	1991
HYBRID PERPETUALS						
Baron Girod de l'Ain	snow	base	snow	−24	−31	1990 (G)
				−28	−33	1991 (G)
Frau Karl Druschki	<1/2	base	base			
Mme. Scipion Cochet	<1/2	base	snow			
Mrs. John Laing	snow	base	snow	(I)	(I)	1991
Reine des Violettes	none	>1/2	snow			
HYBRID RUGOSAS						
Agnes	none	tip	none	−40+	−40+	1991
Amelia Gravereaux	snow	>1/2	snow	(I)	(I)	1991
Belle Poitevine	tip	<1/2	<1/2	−32	−36	1991
Blanc Double de Coubert	none	>1/2	snow	−34	−37	1990 (G)
Bonavista	snow	<1/2	snow			
Charles Albanel	—	base	none	−40	−40	1991
David Thompson	—	—	tip	−32	−36	1991
Delicata	none	base	<1/2			
Elmira	snow	<1/2	snow			
Frau Dagmar Hartopp	none	<1/2	<1/2	−34	−37	1990 (G)
				−38	−39	1991
George Will	none	<1/2	<1/2	(I)	(I)	1991
Grootendorst Supreme	tip	>1/2	>1/2			
Hansa	none	<1/2	<1/2	−28	−33	1990 (G)
				−40+	−40+	1991
				−38	−39	1991
Henry Hudson	tip	<1/2	none	−36	−38	1991
Hunter	snow	base	snow	(I)	(I)	1991
Jens Munk	—	—	none	−36	−38	1994
Martin Frobisher	none	tip	>1/2	(I)	(I)	1991
				−22	−30	1991
				(I)	(I)	1994
Moncton	snow	>1/2	snow			
Mrs. John McNabb	none	tip	<1/2			
Pink Grootendorst	none	base	snow			
Rose à Parfum de l'Hay	none	base	snow			
Rugosa Magnifica	none	none	none	−24	−31	1990 (G)
				−34	−37	1991
Sir Thomas Lipton	tip	<1/2	<1/2	−30	−34	1990 (G)
				−34	−37	1991 (G)
				(I)	(I)	1991
				(I)	(I)	1994
Thérèse Bauer	tip	>1/2	tip			
Thérèse Bugnet	none	none	<1/2	−20	−29	1990 (G)
				−34	−37	1991
Will Alderman	tip	<1/2	tip			

| CULTIVAR | WINTER INJURY | | | MID-WINTER HARDINESS RATING | | YEAR |
	1988-89	1989-90	1990-91	Fahrenheit	Celsius	
HYBRID SPINOSISSIMAS						
Frühlingsanfang	tip	<1/2	>1/2	(I)	(I)	1994
Frühlingsduft	none	>1/2	tip	(I)	(I)	1991
				(I)	(I)	1994
Frühlingsgold	tip	>1/2	>1/2	(I)	(I)	1991
				(I)	(I)	1994
Karl Förster	<1/2	>1/2	tip	(I)	(I)	1991
Suzanne	—	none	none	−44	−42	1991
Wildenfelsgelb	none	tip	>1/2	(I)	(I)	1991
HYBRID SUFFULTAS						
Assiniboine	none	tip	<1/2	−38	−39	1991
Cuthbert Grant	>1/2	base	snow	(I)	(I)	1991
KORDESIIS						
Alexander von Humboldt	none	base	snow			
Dortmund	snow	base	snow	−26	−32	1990 (G)
				−30	−34	1991 (G)
Henry Kelsey	—	—	tip	(I)	(I)	1994
Illusion	snow	base	snow			
John Cabot	none	<1/2	<1/2	(I)	(I)	1991
				(I)	(I)	1994
John Davis	—	—	tip	−22	−30	1994

The Hybrid Musk 'Ballerina' suffers extensive cane injury every winter but comes back vigorously to bloom profusely. The single flowers are borne in large panicles.

CULTIVAR	WINTER INJURY			MID-WINTER HARDINESS RATING		YEAR
	1988-89	1989-90	1990-91	Fahrenheit	Celsius	
Karlsruhe	snow	base	snow			
Parkdirektor Riggers	—	—	<1/2			
Rote Max Graf	snow	base	snow			
William Baffin	none	none	none	−26	−32	1994
MISCELLANEOUS OLD GARDEN ROSES						
Juno	—	>1/2	snow			
MOSSES						
Black Boy	snow	>1/2	snow			
Capitaine John Ingram	none	<1/2	snow			
Chevreul	<1/2	base	snow			
Communis	none	<1/2	<1/2			
Comtesse de Murinais	snow	>1/2	snow			
Deuil de Paul Fontaine	snow	base	snow	(I)	(I)	1990 (G)
Duchess de Verneuil	tip	>1/2	snow			
Gabriel Noyelle	snow	base	snow			
Général Kléber	snow	>1/2	snow			
Gloire des Mousseuses	snow	base	snow			
Goethe	tip	>1/2	snow			
Gracilis	tip	<1/2	snow			
Henri Martin	none	>1/2	<1/2			
Jeanne de Montfort	snow	base	snow			
Julie de Mersan	none	<1/2	snow			
Laneii	tip	>1/2	<1/2			
Louis Gimard	<1/2	>1/2	<1/2			
Mme. de la Rôche-Lambert	none	>1/2	snow			
Mme. Louis Lévêque	snow	base	snow			
Mossman	none	base	tip			
Nuits de Young	none	>1/2	snow	−26	−32	1990 (G)
OEillet Panacheé	none	base	tip			
Perpetual White Moss	snow	base	snow			
Robert Léopold	none	<1/2	snow			
Salet	snow	>1/2	snow	−20	−29	1990 (G)
				−30	−34	1991 (G)
				(I)	(I)	1991
Violacée	none	<1/2	snow			
Waldtraut Nielsen	tip	base	snow			
White Bath	none	base	snow			
William Lobb	<1/2	base	snow	−26	−32	1990 (G)
SHRUB ROSES						
A. MacKenzie	—	—	tip	(I)	(I)	1994
Adelaide Hoodless	>1/2	<1/2	snow	(I)	(I)	1990 (G)
				(I)	(I)	1991
				(I)	(I)	1994
Alchymist	snow	base	snow			
Amiga Mia	—	—	base			
Applejack	tip	tip	<1/2			
Blue Boy	>1/2	base	base			
Bonica	snow	base	snow	(I)	(I)	1991

CULTIVAR	WINTER INJURY			MID-WINTER HARDINESS RATING		YEAR
	1988-89	1989-90	1990-91	Fahrenheit	Celsius	
Carefree Beauty	snow	>1/2	snow	(I)	(I)	1991
				(I)	(I)	1994
Chamcook	none	tip	none			
Champlain	—	—	snow	(I)	(I)	1994
Country Dancer	—	—	base			
Golden Wings	>1/2	base	snow	(I)	(I)	1991
Haidee	none	none	none	−36	−38	1994
J. P. Connell	—	—	none			
John Franklin	snow	base	base			
Lillian Gibson	none	tip	<1/2	(I)	(I)	1991
Morden Amorette	none	<1/2	snow			
Morden Cardinette	—	—	base			
Morden Centennial	<1/2	>1/2	<1/2	(I)	(I)	1991
				(I)	(I)	1994
Morden Ruby	—	—	tip	(I)	(I)	1994
Prairie Dawn	none	none	<1/2	(I)	(I)	1991
				−33	−36	1994
Prairie Princess	—	—	>1/2	(I)	(I)	1991
Prairie Wren	none	>1/2	none	−33	−36	1994
Prairie Youth	tip	none	tip			
Robusta	—	—	>1/2	(I)	(I)	1994
Scharlachglut	tip	>1/2	snow	(I)	(I)	1991
				(I)	(I)	1994
Summer Wind	—	—	snow	−26	−32	1990
				−30	−34	1991
Von Scharnhorst	tip	>1/2	snow			
SPECIES						
Dr. Merkeley	none	<1/2	tip			
R. ambylotis	base	none	none	−40+	−40+	1991
				−44	−42	1993
R. arkansana	—	none	none			
R. canina	tip	none	none			
R. cinnamomea	none	tip	<1/2	−44	−42	1993
R. foetida	—	none	<1/2			
R. foetida bicolor	none	none	>1/2	(I)	(I)	1990 (G)
				(I)	(I)	1991
R. glauca	none	none	tip	−26	−32	1991
				−27	−33	1993
				−33	−36	1993
R. hugonis	<1/2	none	tip	−30	−34	1991
				−22	−30	1993
R. laxa	none	tip	none	−38	−39	1993
R. macounii	—	<1/2	none	−38	−39	1991
				−27	−33	1993
R. mollis	none	<1/2	tip	−27	−33	1993
R. multiflora	snow	>1/2	base	(I)	(I)	1993
R. nitida	none	tip	none	−42	−41	1991
				−38	−39	1993
R. palustris	—	base	none	−38	−39	1993

CULTIVAR	WINTER INJURY			MID-WINTER HARDINESS RATING		YEAR
	1988-89	1989-90	1990-91	Fahrenheit	Celsius	
R. pendulina	none	<1/2	none	−40	−40	1991
				−33	−36	1993
R. pomifera	tip	tip	<1/2	−24	−31	1991
				−22	−30	1993
R. primula	none	none	none	−34	−37	1991 (G)
				−34	−37	1991
				−27	−33	1993
R. rugosa	none	>1/2	none			
R. rugosa alba plena	none	<1/2	none			
R. rugosa kamtchatica	snow	none	none	−44	−42	1993
R. sertata	tip	none	<1/2	−24	−31	1991
				−22	−30	1993
R. setigera	none	>1/2	tip	−30	−34	1991
				−27	−33	1993
R. spinosissima altaica	none	none	none	−42	−41	1991
				−33	−36	1993
R. virginiana	none	<1/2	none	−38	−39	1993
R. woodsii	<1/2	none	none	−30	−34	1991
				−44	−42	1993

R. setigera, *the Prairie Rose, blooms later than other roses, displaying its deep pink flowers in mid-July. Because it produces long winter-hardy canes, the Prairie Rose can be used as a climbing rose.*

Table 5. Winter injury observations and mid-winter hardiness levels (1992-93) for recently planted rose species, some of which were not included in the main evaluation.

Hardiness Rating:
The hardiness rating is the lowest temperature at which 50 percent of the stem sections were uninjured. The designation "(I)" under the Fahrenheit and Celsius columns indicates that the canes were injured in the field prior to collection.

CULTIVAR	WINTER INJURY	HARDINESS RATING	
		Fahrenheit	Celsius
R. acicularis	tip	−44	−42
R. agrestis	snow	−12	−25
R. albertii *	snow	(I)	(I)
R. albertii *	<1/2	(I)	(I)
R. amblyotis	tip	−44	−42
R. arkansana	tip	−38	−39
R. beggariana *	<1/2	−22	−30
R. beggariana *	<1/2	(I)	(I)
R. beggariana *	<1/2	(I)	(I)
R. blanda	tip	−33	−36
R. canina	snow	(I)	(I)
R. carolina	snow	(I)	(I)
R. carolina grandiflora	<1/2	−33	−36
R. cinnamomea	none	−44	−42
R. corymbifera	snow	(I)	(I)
R. elliptica	<1/2	(I)	(I)
R. foliosa	snow	(I)	(I)
R. glauca *	tip	−27	−33
R. glauca *	tip	−33	−36
R. helenae	snow	(I)	(I)
R. hissarica	snow	(I)	(I)
R. hugonis	<1/2	−22	−30
R. jundzlii	>1/2	(I)	(I)
R. kokanica	snow	(I)	(I)
R. laxa	none	−38	−39
R. macounii	tip	−27	−33
R. marrettii	snow	(I)	(I)
R. mollis	tip	−27	−33
R. multiflora	snow	(I)	(I)
R. nitida	tip	−38	−39
R. palustris	tip	−38	−39
R. pendulina	tip	−33	−36
R. pomifera	<1/2	−22	−30
R. primula	tip	−27	−33
R. roxburghii	snow	(I)	(I)
R. rubiginosa	<1/2	(I)	(I)
R. rugosa kamtchatica	none	−44	−42
R. sertata	<1/2	−22	−30
R. setigera	tip	−27	−33
R. spinosissima altaica	none	−33	−36
R. virginiana	tip	−38	−39
R. wilmottiae	<1/2	−22	−30
R. woodsii	none	−44	−42

* Genetically different specimens of species were evaluated and are listed separately

Winter Hardiness Comparisons of Field and Container-Grown Roses

Comparisons of mid-winter hardiness levels of container-grown plants in the overwintering greenhouse and field-grown plants for each of five cultivars and one species were attempted. Canes were sampled in January of 1991. As expected from previous years' observations, the field-grown plant of *R. primula* was uninjured while field-grown plants of each cultivar were already injured at the time of sampling.

The canes of the container-grown *R. primula* were found to be uninjured, and their hardiness level was identical to that of the canes of the field-grown plant.

Canes of each of the five container-grown cultivars were also uninjured. Hardiness levels among the container-grown cultivars ranged from –30° F (–34° C) to –34° F (–37° C). This indicated that all five cultivars possessed adequate mid-winter hardiness to survive the low temperature for the winter of 1990-91 (–24° F, –31° C), which had already occurred on December 26, 1990. The injury to canes of the field-grown cultivars probably occured when plants acclimated too slowly for the early temperature declines of 1990.

Table 6. Comparison of mid-winter hardiness levels between field-grown and container-grown plants of six selected rose taxa. Field injury descriptions are defined on pages 24–25. The designation "(I)" for the Fahrenheit (°F) and Celsius (°C) columns under "field plant" indicates that the canes were injured in the field prior to collection.

CULTIVAR	CLASS	FIELD INJURY	HARDINESS RATING	
			FIELD PLANT	CONTAINER PLANT
Mme. Legras de St. Germain	Alba	snow	(I)	–32°F (–36°C)
Léda	Damask	snow	(I)	–30°F (–34°C)
Mme. Hardy	Damask	>1/2	(I)	–32°F (–36°C)
Sir Thomas Lipton	Hybrid Rugosa	<1/2	(I)	–34°F (–37°C)
Salet	Moss	snow	(I)	–30°F (–34°C)
R. primula	Species	none	–33°F (–37°C)	–33°F (–37°C)

Hardiest Selections

When selecting roses for gardens in cold climates, some winter injury should be expected. Three years of winter injury observations show that even among the hardiest of roses, the number of cultivars or species at the Minnesota Landscape Arboretum which survive winters with little or no cane injury is very limited. Many of these are cultivars ('Alika', 'Betty Bland', 'Harison's Yellow', 'Aylsham', 'Metis', 'Suzanne', 'A. MacKenzie', 'Haidee', 'J. P. Connell', 'Prairie Wren', and 'Prairie Youth') or species that have only one season of bloom or very slight levels of rebloom.

As a group, the Hybrid Rugosa cultivars best combine cane hardiness and moderate or heavy levels of repeat bloom, although winter injury among the Hybrid Rugosas at the Minnesota Landscape Arboretum was more severe than expected. During the evaluation period, the Hybrid Rugosas suffered severe insect infestations of a cynipid wasp gall (*Diplolepsis spinosa*) and the rose stem borer (*Agrilus aurichalceus*), both of which cause galls that stress plants. Reduced hardiness levels may have resulted from these stresses.

Three Kordesii cultivars, 'Henry Kelsey', 'John Davis', and 'William Baffin', also combine cane hardiness with the ability to repeat bloom.

Among other cultivars with moderate to high levels of rebloom, there are many that suffer winter injury, often to the snowline or to the base of the plant, and then regrow vigorously in spring. Because these cultivars bloom on the current year's growth as well as on previous years' wood, they are still attractive flowering plants in the landscape. Plant size is affected rather than flowering ability. Some of these cultivars are 'Chuckles', 'Dapple Dawn', 'Eutin', 'Nearly Wild', 'Redcoat', 'Earth Song', 'Ballerina', 'Cuthbert Grant', 'John Cabot', 'Karlsruhe', 'Parkdirektor Riggers', 'Adelaide Hoodless', 'Amiga Mia', 'Applejack', 'Carefree Beauty', 'Champlain', 'Country Dancer', 'Golden Wings', 'John Franklin', 'Morden Amorette', 'Morden Centennial', 'Morden Ruby', 'Prairie Dawn', 'Prairie Princess', 'Robusta', and 'Summer Wind'.

Severe winter injury is more detrimental to the performance of Old Garden Rose and Shrub Rose cultivars that bloom once in spring on previous years' wood. If winter dieback occurs to the base of the plant, these cultivars will not flower in the spring.

Dieback to the snowline is also detrimental to the largest of these one-time-blooming cultivars since the flowers that occur on the previous years' wood are often "buried" beneath the vigorous growth of new canes in spring. The floral display is better on those large cultivars whose winter injury pattern varies from cane to cane within the crown ($<^1/_2$ and $>^1/_2$ in Table 4). Flowers on the canes that suffered little dieback are still beautifully displayed as the surrounding canes that were injured regrow vigorously from below.

The floral display on the shortest of the one-time-blooming cultivars, such as the Gallicas, is not as severely affected as that of the larger cultivars. During winters with constant snowcover, a smaller proportion of their crowns are lost to winter injury, allowing mature heights to be regained in the following growing season without burying the floral display.

A portion of the Gallica section of the Shrub Rose Garden at the Minnesota Landscape Arboretum.

Plant Size and Habit

The plant size and habit of Old Garden Roses and Shrub Roses differ from those of Hybrid Teas, Floribundas, and other roses with the China Rose predominant in their ancestry. Old Garden Roses and Shrub Roses are true shrubs, typically larger and much more branched in crown architecture.

Among the Old Garden Roses, Albas are the largest specimens, usually 6 feet or greater in height. At the other extreme are the Gallicas, typically 4 feet or shorter and very upright in habit. In between are the Centifolias and Damasks, both of which are more lax in form, and the Moss Roses, more upright in form.

Size is more variable among the rose species and Shrub Rose cultivars. Most plants fall between 3 and 6 feet in height. Some of the tallest plants are found among the Hybrid Spinosissimas, Kordesiis, Shrubs, and Species, with heights ranging up to 12 feet.

Winter's Effect on Size and Habit

Winter injury has a major impact on plant size among roses at the Minnesota Landscape Arboretum. Mature heights are often less than those published in descriptive texts. Most affected are the taller cultivars that lack cane hardiness and commonly die back to the snowline. Even when regrowth is vigorous, many of these plants fail to reach their mature height during the following growing season.

Lower-growing cultivars, such as the Gallicas, with mature heights of 3 to 4 feet, are not as affected by winter injury. A smaller proportion of their crowns are winter-injured and these cultivars can easily regrow to their mature heights the following growing season.

Descriptors for Growth Habits of Rose Cultivars

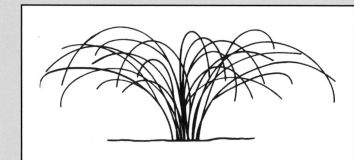

arching . . . . . . Growth is similar to the "spreading" form but cane tips bend back towards the ground .

climbing . . . . . These cultivars produce long canes that, when tied or supported, will climb indefinitely. If not supported, these plants take on a wide arching habit.

dense . . . . Many upright canes create an erect dense plant habit.

groundcover . . . . . Canes grow horizontally over the ground's surface.

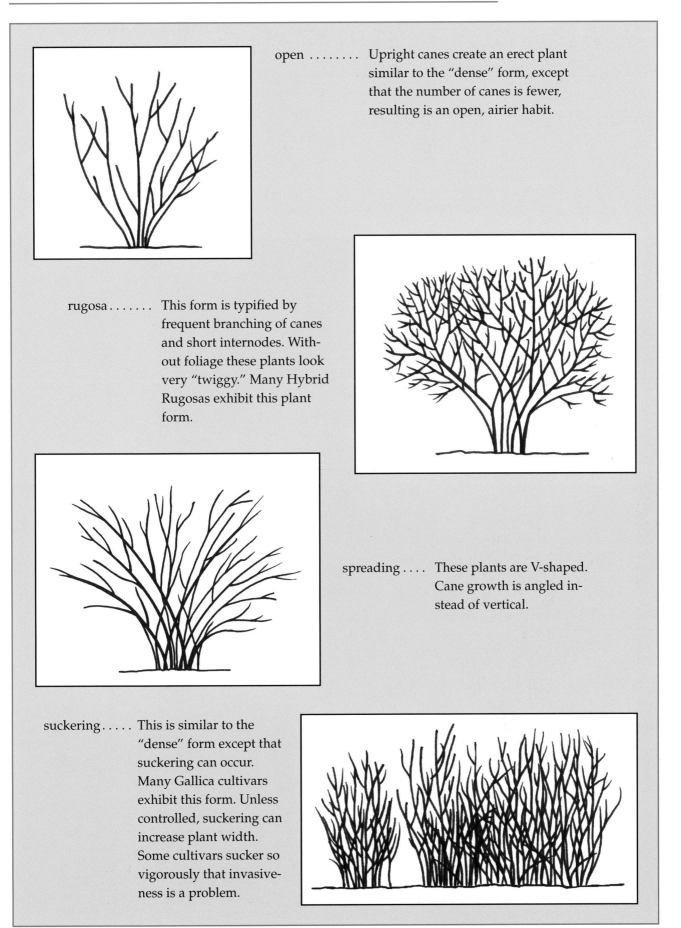

open . . . . Upright canes create an erect plant similar to the "dense" form, except that the number of canes is fewer, resulting is an open, airier habit.

rugosa . . . . This form is typified by frequent branching of canes and short internodes. Without foliage these plants look very "twiggy." Many Hybrid Rugosas exhibit this plant form.

spreading . . . . These plants are V-shaped. Cane growth is angled instead of vertical.

suckering . . . . . This is similar to the "dense" form except that suckering can occur. Many Gallica cultivars exhibit this form. Unless controlled, suckering can increase plant width. Some cultivars sucker so vigorously that invasiveness is a problem.

Snowcover affects rose size and habit in two ways. It is a natural insulator of rose canes, serving to minimize dieback from low winter temperatures. A heavy snow can also weigh canes down, resulting in a wider, flatter plant habit the following growing season.

Andersonii has beautiful, glistening pink, single flowers which bloom on previous year's wood. Its canes are not hardy and need winter protection for flowering to occur.

Plant Width

A rose plant's width is most often affected by a cultivar's ability to sucker. Suckering is common among Old Garden Roses and Species Roses.

Most rose cultivars are propagated by budding. Because the bud union is susceptible to winter injury, plants in northern climates should be planted with the bud union 2 to 4 inches below ground to protect the union from injury. This often results in the formation of roots by the cultivar above the bud union so that plants go "own-root" over time, and suckering can become a problem. Unless controlled, roses prone to suckering will continue to increase in width and invade the space occupied by neighboring plants.

Kordesiis commonly produce extremely long canes in a short period of time and are often trained as climbing roses. In Minnesota, inadequate cane hardiness prevents most of these roses from being used as climbers. Instead, they are grown as shrubs with long, arching canes. Because of their rampant cane growth, they measure among some of the widest cultivars.

Plant size and form are described in Table 7. The heights and widths listed are the maximum sizes that were seen at the Arboretum between 1989 and 1992. Eight terms were used to describe plant form for each cultivar or species: arching, climbing, dense, groundcover, open, rugosa, spreading or suckering (see pages 42 and 43).

Table 7. Plant sizes and growing habits of the rose cultivars and species evaluated at the Minnesota Landscape Arboretum. Arrangement is alphabetical by and within classes.

CULTIVAR	YEAR PLANTED	HEIGHT (FEET)	WIDTH	HEIGHT (METERS)	WIDTH	HABIT
ALBAS						
Alba semi-plena	1959	6.0	10.0	1.8	3.0	suckering
Belle Amour	1967	4.5	7.0	1.4	2.1	suckering
Chloris	1965	7.0	6.5	2.1	2.0	suckering
Jeanne d'Arc	1972	5.0	6.0	1.5	1.8	dense
Königin von Dänemark	1963	3.0	2.5	0.9	0.8	dense
Mme. Legras de St. Germain	1965	3.0	3.5	0.9	1.1	open
Pompon Blanc Parfait	1963	4.0	6.0	1.2	1.8	suckering
BOURBONS						
Gipsy Boy	1967	5.5	8.5	1.7	2.6	arching
Mme. Ernest Calvat	1978	4.5	9.0	1.4	2.7	arching
CENTIFOLIAS						
Blanchefleur	1967	5.5	8.0	1.7	2.4	suckering
Bullata	1963	3.5	5.0	1.1	1.5	open
Cabbage Rose	1965	6.0	10.0	1.8	3.0	suckering
Centifolia Variegata	1978	4.5	6.5	1.4	2.0	open
Fantin-Latour	1973	4.0	9.0	1.2	2.7	arching

CULTIVAR	YEAR PLANTED	HEIGHT (FEET)	WIDTH	HEIGHT (METERS)	WIDTH	HABIT
Petite de Hollande	1963	4.0	3.5	1.2	1.1	dense
Prolifera de Redouté	1965	3.0	5.5	0.9	1.7	suckering
Red Provence	1965	2.5	5.0	0.8	1.5	open
Rose de Meaux	1963	1.0	1.0	0.3	0.3	dense
Rose des Peintres	1967	2.5	4.5	0.8	1.4	open
Tour de Malakoff	1963	3.0	3.5	0.9	1.1	suckering
DAMASKS						
Autumn Damask	1961	4.5	6.0	1.4	1.8	suckering
Césonie	1967	5.5	6.5	1.7	2.0	spreading
Kazanlik	1972	4.0	5.0	1.2	1.5	open
Léda	1963	2.5	6.5	0.8	2.0	suckering
Mme. Hardy	1959	6.0	7.0	1.8	2.1	suckering
Marie Louise	1963	4.0	6.0	1.2	1.8	suckering
Omar Khayyám	1972	3.0	3.5	0.9	1.1	open
Rose de Rescht	1975	3.5	3.5	1.1	1.1	suckering
St. Nicholas	1963	3.0	4.5	0.9	1.4	suckering
York and Lancaster	1973	6.0	8.0	1.8	2.4	spreading
FLORIBUNDAS						
Chuckles	1987	2.0	4.0	0.6	1.2	spreading
Dapple Dawn	1989	3.5	4.5	1.1	1.4	dense
Eutin	1990	3.0	3.5	0.9	1.1	open
Nearly Wild	1980	3.0	5.0	0.9	1.5	rugosa
Redcoat	1986	4.5	4.5	1.4	1.4	dense
GALLICAS						
Alain Blanchard	1963	4.0	6.5	1.2	2.0	suckering
Alice Vena	1967	4.0	6.0	1.2	1.8	suckering
Alika	1967	8.0	12.0	2.4	3.7	suckering
Belle des Jardins	1963	2.5	6.5	0.8	2.0	suckering
Belle Isis	1967	4.5	7.0	1.4	2.1	arching
Cardinal de Richelieu	1965	4.0	5.0	1.2	1.5	suckering
Charles de Mills	1963	4.0	5.5	1.2	1.7	suckering
Désireé Parmentier	1965	5.5	6.5	1.7	2.0	suckering
Duchesse de Montebello	1975	5.0	3.0	1.5	0.9	dense
Narcisse de Salvandy	1967	7.0	10.0	2.1	3.0	spreading
Président de Sèze	1963	4.0	12.0	1.2	3.7	suckering
Rosa Mundi	1965	3.5	4.0	1.1	1.2	suckering
Rose du Maître d'École	1963	4.0	6.0	1.2	1.8	suckering
Superb Tuscan	1985	4.0	6.5	1.2	2.0	suckering
Tuscany	1965	4.0	3.0	1.2	0.9	dense
GRANDIFLORAS						
Earth Song	1986	3.0	3.0	0.9	0.9	open
HYBRID ALBAS						
Mme. Plantier	1975	5.0	5.0	1.5	1.5	dense

CULTIVAR	YEAR PLANTED	HEIGHT (FEET)	WIDTH	HEIGHT (METERS)	WIDTH	HABIT
HYBRID BLANDAS						
Betty Bland	1963	5.5	7.0	1.7	2.1	suckering
HYBRID CANINAS						
Andersonii	1987	5.5	12.0	1.7	3.7	arching
HYBRID FOETIDAS						
Harison's Yellow	1970	6.5	11.0	2.0	3.4	suckering
HYBRID MOYESIIS						
Marguerite Hilling	1965	8.0	8.0	2.4	2.4	arching
Nevada	1963	5.5	6.5	1.7	2.0	arching
HYBRID MUSKS						
Ballerina	1990	3.5	4.5	1.1	1.4	arching
Belinda	1972	2.0	3.5	0.6	1.1	spreading
Daphne	1972	3.5	7.0	1.1	2.1	arching
Will Scarlet	1978	3.5	4.0	1.1	1.2	open
HYBRID NITIDAS						
Aylsham	1976	4.0	5.0	1.2	1.5	dense
Metis	1970	5.0	6.0	1.5	1.8	suckering
HYBRID PERPETUALS						
Baron Girod de l'Ain	1978	4.0	4.0	1.2	1.2	open
Frau Karl Druschki	1978	4.5	6.0	1.4	1.8	open
Mme. Scipion Cochet	1978	3.0	4.0	0.9	1.2	open
Mrs. John Laing	1963	4.0	5.0	1.2	1.5	open
Reine des Violettes	1959	3.0	3.0	0.9	0.9	open
HYBRID RUGOSAS						
Agnes	1988	5.0	5.0	1.5	1.5	rugosa
Amelia Gravereaux	1960	4.0	7.0	1.2	2.1	open
Belle Poitevine	1963	2.5	5.0	0.8	1.5	rugosa
Blanc Double de Coubert	1959	2.5	2.5	0.8	0.8	rugosa
Bonavista	1980	5.0	6.0	1.5	1.8	spreading
Charles Albanel	1985	2.0	4.0	0.6	1.2	rugosa
David Thompson	1988	5.5	6.5	1.7	2.0	arching
Delicata	1963	3.0	4.0	0.9	1.2	rugosa
Elmira	1980	4.0	5.0	1.2	1.5	spreading
Frau Dagmar Hartopp	1972	2.5	4.0	0.8	1.2	rugosa
George Will	1966	4.0	4.5	1.2	1.4	dense
Grootendorst Supreme	1963	4.0	5.5	1.2	1.7	dense
Hansa	1954	4.0	5.5	1.2	1.7	rugosa
Henry Hudson	1980	4.5	7.0	1.4	2.1	rugosa
Hunter	1980	3.0	5.0	0.9	1.5	open
Jens Munk	1988	5.0	5.0	1.5	1.5	dense
Martin Frobisher	1969	5.0	6.0	1.5	1.8	dense

CULTIVAR	YEAR PLANTED	HEIGHT (FEET)	WIDTH	HEIGHT (METERS)	WIDTH	HABIT
Moncton	1980	4.0	4.5	1.2	1.4	spreading
Mrs. John McNabb	1965	5.5	8.0	1.7	2.4	spreading
Pink Grootendorst	1965	3.0	4.5	0.9	1.4	dense
Rose À Parfum de l'Hay	1963	5.0	5.0	1.5	1.5	dense
Rugosa Magnifica	1988	4.0	6.0	1.2	1.8	rugosa
Sir Thomas Lipton	1986	5.0	6.0	1.5	1.8	arching
Thérèse Bauer	1967	2.5	4.0	0.8	1.2	open
Thérèse Bugnet	1965	5.0	5.5	1.5	1.7	open
Will Alderman	1963	4.0	3.5	1.2	1.1	dense
HYBRID SPINOSISSIMAS						
Frühlingsanfang	1965	5.5	8.0	1.7	2.4	arching
Frühlingsduft	1963	7.0	8.5	2.1	2.6	spreading
Frühlingsgold	1978	8.0	11.0	2.4	3.4	arching
Karl Förster	1978	4.5	6.0	1.4	1.8	spreading
Suzanne	1956	5.5	7.0	1.7	2.1	suckering
Wildenfelsgelb	1965	6.0	7.0	1.8	2.1	spreading

Mutations or sports resulting in changes of plant appearance are common among all roses. 'Marguerite Hilling' is a pink sport or mutation of 'Nevada'. The cultivars are identical except for flower color. A branch of this 'Marguerite Hilling' is reverting to the white-flowered 'Nevada'.

CULTIVAR	YEAR PLANTED	HEIGHT WIDTH (FEET)		HEIGHT WIDTH (METERS)		HABIT
HYBRID SUFFULTAS						
Assiniboine	1970	4.0	6.5	1.2	2.0	dense
Cuthbert Grant	1968	4.0	5.0	1.2	1.5	spreading
KORDESIIS						
Alexander von Humboldt	1975	5.0	5.0	1.5	1.5	climbing
Dortmund	1965	4.0	11.0	1.2	3.4	climbing
Henry Kelsey	1989	4.5	10.0	1.4	3.0	climbing
Illusion	1965	4.0	6.5	1.2	2.0	climbing
John Cabot	1979	6.0	8.0	1.8	2.4	spreading
John Davis	1992	5.0	6.0	1.5	1.8	dense
Karlsruhe	1965	2.0	5.5	0.6	1.7	climbing
Parkdirektor Riggers	1990	6.5	9.0	2.0	2.7	climbing
Rote Max Graf	1987	2.5	8.0	0.8	2.4	groundcover
William Baffin	1988	7.5	10.0	2.3	3.0	spreading
MISCELLANEOUS OLD GARDEN ROSES						
Juno	1972	4.5	6.5	1.4	2.0	open
MOSSES						
Black Boy	1963	6.0	7.0	1.8	2.1	suckering
Capitaine John Ingram	1967	4.0	7.0	1.2	2.1	suckering
Chevreul	1967	4.5	5.0	1.4	1.5	dense
Communis	1959	7.0	7.0	2.1	2.1	suckering
Comtesse de Murinais	1963	5.0	5.0	1.5	1.5	dense
Deuil de Paul Fontaine	1959	4.0	5.0	1.2	1.5	open
Duchess de Verneuil	1967	4.5	5.0	1.4	1.5	dense
Gabriel Noyelle	1963	6.0	6.0	1.8	1.8	open
Général Kléber	1965	3.5	6.0	1.1	1.8	suckering
Gloire des Mousseuses	1959	3.0	3.0	0.9	0.9	dense
Goethe	1967	6.0	6.0	1.8	1.8	suckering
Gracilis	1967	3.5	5.5	1.1	1.7	suckering
Henri Martin	1959	5.0	10.0	1.5	3.0	spreading
Jeanne de Montfort	1959	5.5	5.0	1.7	1.5	dense
Julie de Mersan	1965	4.0	6.0	1.2	1.8	suckering
Laneii	1967	5.0	4.0	1.5	1.2	dense
Louis Gimard	1965	4.0	6.0	1.2	1.8	suckering
Mme. de la Rôche-Lambert	1967	5.0	4.0	1.5	1.2	dense
Mme. Louis Lévêque	1967	5.0	5.0	1.5	1.5	suckering
Mossman	1963	5.0	5.0	1.5	1.5	open
Nuits de Young	1963	6.0	6.5	1.8	2.0	suckering
OEillet Panacheé	1967	4.0	5.0	1.2	1.5	dense
Perpetual White Moss	1967	3.0	4.0	0.9	1.2	dense
Robert Léopold	1967	4.0	5.0	1.2	1.5	dense
Salet	1959	5.0	6.0	1.5	1.8	dense
Violacée	1975	4.0	6.0	1.2	1.8	suckering
Waldtraut Nielsen	1967	7.0	5.0	2.1	1.5	dense
White Bath	1965	5.5	6.5	1.7	2.0	suckering
William Lobb	1967	6.0	8.0	1.8	2.4	spreading

CULTIVAR	YEAR PLANTED	HEIGHT (FEET)	WIDTH	HEIGHT (METERS)	WIDTH	HABIT
SHRUB ROSES						
A. MacKenzie	1990	6.0	5.5	1.8	1.7	arching
Adelaide Hoodless	1987	5.5	6.5	1.7	2.0	spreading
Alchymist	1986	4.0	11.0	1.2	3.4	climbing
Amiga Mia	1986	3.5	3.5	1.1	1.1	dense
Applejack	1975	6.0	9.0	1.8	2.7	spreading
Blue Boy	1963	4.0	3.0	1.2	0.9	spreading
Bonica	1987	2.5	4.0	0.8	1.2	spreading
Carefree Beauty	1988	4.0	4.0	1.2	1.2	spreading
Chamcook	1966	2.0	4.5	0.6	1.4	suckering
Champlain	1987	3.0	2.5	0.9	0.8	spreading
Country Dancer	1986	2.5	3.5	0.8	1.1	dense
Golden Wings	1987	5.0	4.5	1.5	1.4	dense
Haidee	1963	8.0	12.0	2.4	3.7	spreading
J. P. Connell	1992	5.5	3.5	1.7	1.1	spreading
John Franklin	1988	3.0	4.0	0.9	1.2	dense
Lillian Gibson	1963	9.0	11.0	2.7	3.4	arching
Morden Amorette	1987	4.0	5.0	1.2	1.5	spreading
Morden Cardinette	1992	2.5	1.0	0.8	0.3	open
Morden Centennial	1987	5.5	4.5	1.7	1.4	dense
Morden Ruby	1989	3.5	5.0	1.1	1.5	spreading
Prairie Dawn	1960	8.0	10.0	2.4	3.0	arching
Prairie Princess	1986	5.5	6.5	1.7	2.0	open
Prairie Wren	1955	8.0	12.0	2.4	3.7	spreading
Prairie Youth	1955	10.0	13.0	3.0	4.0	arching
Robusta	1990	5.0	5.5	1.5	1.7	dense
Scharlachglut	1967	7.0	7.5	2.1	2.3	dense
Summer Wind	1990	3.0	3.0	0.9	0.9	dense
Von Scharnhorst	1967	4.0	3.0	1.2	0.9	dense
SPECIES						
Dr. Merkeley	1962	5.0	10.0	1.5	3.0	suckering
R. ambylotis	1965	7.0	9.0	2.1	2.7	suckering
R. arkansana	1961	2.5	3.5	0.8	1.1	spreading
R. canina	1960	4.5	6.5	1.4	2.0	arching
R. cinnamomea	1973	3.5	5.5	1.1	1.7	arching
R. foetida	1960	5.5	6.0	1.7	1.8	dense
R. foetida bicolor	1975	5.0	4.5	1.5	1.4	dense
R. glauca	1970	8.0	9.0	2.4	2.7	arching
R. hugonis	1961	6.0	10.0	1.8	3.0	spreading
R. laxa	1953	10.0	12.0	3.0	3.7	arching
R. macounii	1959	6.5	10.5	2.0	3.2	suckering
R. mollis	1960	8.0	11.0	2.4	3.4	suckering
R. multiflora	1988	4.5	12.0	1.4	3.7	arching
R. nitida	1984	3.5	7.0	1.1	2.1	spreading
R. palustris	1972	5.0	9.0	1.5	2.7	dense
R. pendulina	1961	7.0	9.0	2.1	2.7	arching
R. pomifera	1956	6.0	7.0	1.8	2.1	suckering
R. primula	1962	11.0	14.0	3.4	4.3	arching

CULTIVAR	YEAR PLANTED	HEIGHT (FEET)	WIDTH	HEIGHT (METERS)	WIDTH	HABIT
R. rugosa	1957	4.0	6.0	1.2	1.8	rugosa
R. rugosa alba plena	1974	4.0	6.5	1.2	2.0	rugosa
R. rugosa kamtchatica	1986	4.0	6.0	1.2	1.8	rugosa
R. sertata	1963	7.0	7.0	2.1	2.1	dense
R. setigera	1967	5.5	13.0	1.7	4.0	arching
R. spinosissima altaica	1973	4.0	6.0	1.2	1.8	dense
R. virginiana	1967	7.0	9.0	2.1	2.7	arching
R. woodsii	1979	5.5	6.0	1.7	1.8	spreading

'Alika', like most Gallicas, suckers. The clumps seen here were originally a single plant. Flowers are deep pink, semi-double, and very fragrant.

Diseases

Many diseases infect roses. The most common and serious, from an aesthetic standpoint, are foliar diseases. These include blackspot, powdery mildew, leaf spots, and rust. Severe infections of any of these diseases reduce plant vigor. Gardeners who plant roses susceptible to them are ultimately forced to choose between a program of regular fungicide spraying or acceptance of roses as landscape liabilities from mid-summer through autumn.

Blackspot (Diplocarpon rosae)

Blackspot is diagnosed when small, circular, black spots with feathery margins develop on upper leaflet surfaces.[10] Spots are $^1/_8$ to $^1/_2$ inch (2 to 12 mm) in diameter. The leaf tissue surrounding these spots turns

[10] R.K. Horst. *Compendium of Rose Diseases.* APS Press, St. Paul. 1983.

'Adelaide Hoodless' produces brilliant red blooms which cover the plant in June (left). Unfortunately, the cultivar is very susceptible to blackspot. Without fungicidal protection, it can be completely defoliated by mid-summer (right).

yellow and this chlorosis spreads until the leaflet drops from the plant.

Less noticeable black spots can also occur on a plant's petioles, stipules, peduncles, fruit, and sepals (see figure on page 73). Flower petals may be distorted and red flecks may occur. Raised, purple-red blotches that later blacken and blister develop on the immature wood of first-year canes.

Expanding leaves between 6 and 14 days of age are most susceptible to blackspot infection. The optimal temperature for disease development is 75° F (24° C). Conidia, the infecting spores, must be continuously wet for at least seven hours for infection to occur.

The fungus overwinters in infected canes and in fallen leaves. Protective fungicidal sprays and planting of resistant cultivars are the best means of blackspot control.

Slight, moderate, and heavy infections of blackspot are illustrated, top to bottom, in this series of photos.

Powdery Mildew (Sphaerotheca pannosa)

Powdery mildew is another widely distributed and serious disease of roses. Young tissues are the most susceptible and the disease is typically diagnosed when white, powdery patches of fungal growth appear on young leaves. [11] These leaves will often fold inward or become twisted and distorted. New stem growth and flowers can also be attacked.

Optimal conditions for disease development are daytime temperatures between 62° and 77° F (18° to 25° C), with 97 to 99 percent relative

[11] R.K. Horst. *Compendium of Rose Diseases.* APS Press, St. Paul. 1983.

humidity, followed by a night temperature of 60° F (16° C) and a relative humidity of 90 to 99 percent. Although high humidity encourages disease development, powdery mildew will not develop well when leaves and other plant parts are wet. Conidia, the infecting spores, will not germinate in water.

The fungus overwinters in rudimentary leaves in buds or in the inner bud scales. Fungicide sprays provide the best control.

Slight, moderate, and heavy infections of powdery mildew are illustrated, top to bottom, in this series of photos (left).

Slight, moderate, and heavy infections of leaf spots are illustrated, top to bottom, in this series of photos (right).

Leaf Spots

There are several leaf spot diseases of roses, including those caused by *Alternaria, Cercospora, Colletotrichum*, and *Sphaceloma rosarum*. [12]

Spot anthracnose is caused by *Sphaceloma rosarum*. Young spots are red, occasionally brown or purple, and occur on upper leaf surfaces. Spots are circular and up to ¼ inch (.5 cm) in diameter. The center of spots turn gray or white.

[12] R.K. Horst. *Compendium of Rose Diseases.* APS Press, St. Paul. 1983.

The center of the spot often falls out, leaving a shot-hole appearance. Heavy infections of spot anthracnose can result in yellowing of infected leaflets and will cause defoliation.

Conidia are formed in spring and continue to form on rainy days through the growing season. Spores are spread by splashing water.

Rust

Nine species of the rust fungus *Phragmidium* occur on roses.[13] Rust is typically diagnosed when reddish orange pustules, containing spore masses, appear on lower leaf surfaces. As the pustules develop, they appear on the upper leaf surface as chlorotic spots, giving this surface a mottled appearance. At the Minnesota Landscape Arboretum, leaves growing at the base of plants are the most commonly infected.

Temperatures between 64° and 70° F (18° to 21° C) are optimal for rust development. Continuous moisture for two to four hours is necessary for infection to occur.

Rust is not as severe of a problem in Minnesota as it is in the western United States and other areas with wet, cool growing seasons.

Slight, moderate, and heavy infections of rust are illustrated, top to bottom, in this series of photos.

[13] R.K. Horst. *Compendium of Rose Diseases.* APS Press, St. Paul. 1983.

Observing the Diseases

The incidence of blackspot, powdery mildew, leaf spots, and rust was monitored at the Minnesota Landscape Arboretum during the growing seasons of 1990 and 1992. Both of these growing seasons were cool and humid, providing excellent conditions for disease development. [14] The results of these observations are in Table 8.

Roses in the Shrub Rose Garden at the Arboretum are not protected with pesticide sprays, which allowed differences in disease incidence among cultivars to be observed. Observations were made from early August through late September. Disease incidence was recorded as none, slight, moderate, or heavy (see photos on pages 53-55) for each cultivar or species. Levels recorded in Table 8 are the highest seen for the year.

Leaf spot diseases were not differentiated during the observations. Symptoms are similar among several of the leaf spot diseases and literature that aids in differentiating among these diseases is scarce. Most infections appeared to be spot anthracnose.

The degree of infection on a field-grown plant is a function of several factors. A disease-free plant may indicate that the cultivar is resistant to the races of pathogens present, while infected cultivars are susceptible.

[14] Figures in Appendix A show maximum and minimum air temperatures and monthly precipitation for the years 1990 and 1992.

R. pomifera is a Species Rose with small, medium pink flowers. It is grown for its large ornamental hips, which have high Vitamin C content. R. pomifera is disease tolerant at the Minnesota Landscape Arboretum.

Pathogenicity among *Diplocarpon rosae* races has been found to be cultivar dependent. [15]

On the other hand, an uninfected plant may be an "escape," a plant that was missed by infecting spores because of non-uniform pathogen distribution.

Disease development is also affected by environmental variables, such as temperature, humidity, and air circulation. Differing levels of infection may simply represent localized, microclimatic variations that are conducive or detrimental to disease development.

Controlled screening techniques are necessary to separate genetic resistance from these other factors that influence disease development.

Patterns and Trends

Some trends can be seen across evaluation years and among and within classes of roses. The levels of infection for all diseases monitored were generally higher in 1992 than in 1990. The levels of blackspot and powdery mildew on the Species Roses were the exception to this trend, with infections much more severe in 1990 than in 1992.

The year 1992 was a particularly severe one for leaf spot occurrence. Leaf spot infections were more prevalent and more severe among the Old Garden Roses than among other classes.

Rust infections at the Minnesota Landscape Arboretum were the most prevalent and severe among Hybrid Rugosa cultivars.

The Albas and the Damasks were two of the most disease-free groups of Old Garden Roses at the Minnesota Landscape Arboretum. Leaf spots were the most common disease problem. Blackspot and powdery mildew incidence were not common or severe. Rust was not present in either year. 'Königin von Dänemark' and 'Belle Amour' were the most disease-free Albas in 1990 and 1992. 'Césonie', 'Kazanlik', 'Rose de Rescht', 'St. Nicholas', and 'York and Lancaster' were the healthiest Damasks.

Blackspot, powdery mildew, and leaf spots were observed on Centifolias, but rust infections were rare. The most disease-free representative of this class in 1990 and 1992 was 'Centifolia Variegata'.

---

[15] I. Wenefrida and J. A. Spencer. *Marssonina rosae* Variants in Mississippi and Their Virulence on Selected Rose Cultivars. *Plant Disease* 77 (3): 246-248. 1993.

The most prevalent diseases of the Gallicas were powdery mildew and leaf spots. Blackspot and rust infections were minor. The healthiest cultivars in 1990 and 1992 were 'Alain Blanchard', 'Belle Isis', 'Charles de Mills', 'Duchesse de Montebello', 'Narcisse de Salvandy', 'Superb Tuscan', and 'Tuscany'.

Although powdery mildew is often noted as the most common disease of Moss Roses and other Old Garden Roses, blackspot and leaf spots were much more common than powdery mildew on the Moss Roses during the two years of monitoring. Because water on leaves and other plant parts discourages the development of powdery mildew, the higher-than-normal precipitation of 1990 and 1992 may have affected powdery mildew incidence.[16] 'Henri Martin' and 'William Lobb' were completely disease-free in 1990 and 1992. Other healthy Moss Roses were 'Capitaine John Ingram', 'Communis', 'Gracilis', 'Nuits de Young', 'Perpetual White Moss', ' Salet', 'Violacée', 'Waldtraut Nielsen', and 'White Bath'.

When present, the levels of leaf spot, powdery mildew, and black-spot among the Floribundas, Hybrid Moyesiis, Hybrid Perpetuals, Hybrid Spinosissimas, and Kordesiis were higher in 1992 than 1990. Blackspot was the most common and severe disease. The Floribundas were the most disease-free of these classes, bothered only by slight levels of blackspot. The Kordesiis, with their glossy foliage, were also healthy, although moderate levels of blackspot were seen on some cultivars in 1992.

Like their parent species *R. nitida*, 'Aylsham' and 'Metis' are suscep-tible to powdery mildew. When present, disease levels on the two Hybrid Suffultas, 'Assiniboine' and 'Cuthbert Grant', were slight, although 'Assiniboine' is very susceptible to rust.

Hybrid Rugosa cultivars are very resistant to blackspot and pow-dery mildew in comparison to other rose cultivars. Leaf spots can occur but are not common. Rust was the most common disease problem of the group. 'Charles Albanel', 'Frau Dagmar Hartopp', and 'Thérèse Bauer' were disease-free in 1990 and 1992. 'Agnes', 'Blanc Double de Coubert', 'Delicata', 'Grootendorst Supreme', 'Pink Grootendorst', and 'Sir Thomas Lipton' were also very healthy with only light infections of leaf spots or rust.

There are no identifiable trends in disease resistance among the Shrub Roses, probably due to the heterogeneous genetic backgrounds of this group. Diseases do occur, particularily blackspot and leaf spots. Although the summers of 1990 and 1992 provided excellent conditions

---

[16] Figures in Appendix A show maximum and minimum air temperatures and monthly precipitation for the years 1990 and 1992.

for disease development, most infections on the Shrub Roses were slight to moderate. The exceptions to this were 'Adelaide Hoodless' with its high levels of blackspot and leaf spots in 1992; the high levels of blackspot on 'Morden Amorette', 'Morden Cardinette', and 'Morden Ruby' in 1992; and the high level of blackspot on 'Praire Youth' in 1990. 'Applejack' and 'Summer Wind' were disease-free in 1990 and 1992. 'Bonica', 'Care-free Beauty', 'Chamcook', 'Champlain', 'Golden Wings', 'Haidee', 'John Franklin', 'Lillian Gibson', and 'Prairie Wren' were also very healthy.

Species Roses, like the Shrub Roses, usually have slight to moderate levels of disease incidence. *Rosa arkansana* and *R. rugosa kamtchatica* can be noted for their high susceptibility to powdery mildew, and severe infections of blackspot were seen on *R. canina*, *R. foetida*, *R. foetida bicolor*, *R. glauca*, and *R. woodsii* in either or both of the years 1990 and 1992. *Rosa primula* and *R. spinosissima altaica* were disease-free in 1990 and 1992. Other healthy species were *R. amblyotis*, *R. hugonis*, *R. laxa*, *R. mollis*, *R. multiflora*, *R. pomifera*, *R. rugosa*, *R. rugosa alba-plena*, and *R. setigera*.

Table 8. Blackspot, powdery mildew, leaf spots and rust levels during 1990 and 1992 growing seasons. Arrangement is alphabetical by and within classes observations.

Table Designations:
- Blank = disease-free
- S = slight infection
- M = moderate infection
- H = heavy infection
- — = data not taken in 1990 or 1992

CULTIVAR	BLACKSPOT 1990	1992	POWDERY MILDEW 1990	1992	LEAF SPOTS 1990	1992	RUST 1990	1992
ALBAS								
Alba semi-plena					S	M		
Belle Amour						S		
Chloris					S	M		
Jeanne d'Arc					S	M		
Königin von Dänemark								
Mme. Legras de St. Germain	S				S	M		
Pompon Blanc Parfait			S		S	S		
BOURBONS								
Gipsy Boy			S					
Mme. Ernest Calvat		M				S		

CULTIVAR	BLACKSPOT		POWDERY MILDEW		LEAF SPOTS		RUST	
	1990	1992	1990	1992	1990	1992	1990	1992
CENTIFOLIAS								
Blanchefleur			S	M	S	M		
Bullata	M	H						
Cabbage Rose		S		S	S	M		M
Centifolia Variegata						S		
Fantin-Latour			H	H		M		
Petite de Hollande	S				M	M		
Prolifera de Redouté		M	S	H		S		
Red Provence		M				S		
Rose de Meaux		—		—		—		—
Rose des Peintres		H			S			
Tour de Malakoff	M	H	S					
DAMASKS								
Autumn Damask		S	S	S	M			
Césonie						S		
Kazanlik						S		
Léda	M				S	M		
Mme. Hardy					S	H		
Marie Louise				M	M	S		
Omar Khayyám		S				M		
Rose de Rescht	S							
St. Nicholas					S	S		
York and Lancaster		S				S		
FLORIBUNDAS								
Chuckles		S						
Dapple Dawn	—	S	—		—		—	
Eutin	—	M	—		—		—	
Nearly Wild		S				S		
Redcoat	—	M	—	S	—		—	
GALLICAS								
Alain Blanchard						S		S
Alice Vena			H	H	S	S		
Alika			S	S	S	M	M	M
Belle des Jardins				M		M		S
Belle Isis						S		
Cardinal de Richelieu	S	S	S	S				
Charles de Mills			S	M				
Désireé Parmentier		M	S		S	S		
Duchesse de Montebello		—		—		—		—
Narcisse de Salvandy					S	S		
Président de Sèze				M				
Rosa Mundi		—	H	—		—		—
Rose du Maître d'École				M		S		
Superb Tuscan					S	S		
Tuscany		—		—		—		—

CULTIVAR	BLACKSPOT 1990	BLACKSPOT 1992	POWDERY MILDEW 1990	POWDERY MILDEW 1992	LEAF SPOTS 1990	LEAF SPOTS 1992	RUST 1990	RUST 1992
GRANDIFLORAS								
Earth Song	—	M	—		—		—	
HYBRID ALBAS								
Mme. Plantier					S	M		
HYBRID BLANDAS								
Betty Bland	M		H	M		M		M
HYBRID CANINAS								
Andersonii								
HYBRID FOETIDAS								
Harison's Yellow					S	S		
HYBRID MOYESIIS								
Marguerite Hilling	M	M		S				
Nevada		M		S	S			
HYBRID MUSKS								
Ballerina	—		—		—		—	
Belinda		S						
Daphne				S				
Will Scarlet						M		
HYBRID NITIDAS								
Aylsham	S		S	M		M		
Metis			S	M				
HYBRID PERPETUALS								
Baron Girod de l'Ain		M		H				
Frau Karl Druschki		H	M	M				
Mme. Scipion Cohet		H						
Mrs. John Laing	S			S		S		
Reine des Violettes		M						
HYBRID RUGOSAS								
Agnes								S
Amelia Gravereaux						M		H
Belle Poitevine						S		S
Blanc Double de Coubert					S			
Bonavista	M	H			S	H		
Charles Albanel								
David Thompson	—	S	—	M	—		—	
Delicata								S
Elmira	S					H		
Frau Dagmar Hartopp								
George Will			M	M	M	S	S	

CULTIVAR	BLACKSPOT		POWDERY MILDEW		LEAF SPOTS		RUST	
	1990	1992	1990	1992	1990	1992	1990	1992
Grootendorst Supreme								S
Hansa		H						
Henry Hudson					S	S		S
Hunter	S	S					S	S
Jens Munk	—	M	—		—		—	
Martin Frobisher	H	H				M		M
Moncton	S							
Mrs. John McNabb	M		S		M	H	H	H
Pink Grootendorst								S
Rose à Parfum de l'Hay					S	M		S
Rugosa Magnifica								M
Sir Thomas Lipton							S	S
Thérèse Bauer								
Thérèse Bugnet		S	M	M	M	M	M	M
Will Alderman			S					S
HYBRID SPINOSISSIMAS								
Frühlingsanfang		H	S		S	M		
Frühlingsduft	M	H				S		
Frühlingsgold	M	M				S		
Karl Förster			S	M				
Suzanne	S				S	H	S	
Wildenfelsgelb	S	H						
HYBRID SUFFULTAS								
Assiniboine			S		S	S		H
Cuthbert Grant	S		M		S	S	S	
KORDESIIS								
Alexander von Humbolt		M						
Dortmund								
Henry Kelsey	—	M	—		—		—	
Illusion								
John Cabot						S		
John Davis	—		—	H	—	S	—	
Karlsruhe		M			S			
Parkdirektor Riggers		S						
Rote Max Graf								
William Baffin		S				S		
MISCELLANEOUS OLD GARDEN ROSES								
Juno		M	H	H				
MOSSES								
Black Boy	H	H						
Capitaine John Ingram					S	S		
Chevreul	M	H				M		
Communis					S			
Comtesse de Murinais	M					M		S
Deuil de Paul Fontaine	M	S		S	S	H		

CULTIVAR	BLACKSPOT		POWDERY MILDEW		LEAF SPOTS		RUST	
	1990	1992	1990	1992	1990	1992	1990	1992
Duchess de Vereuil			S		M	S		
Gabriel Noyelle		S				H		
Général Kléber	H	M				H		
Gloire des Mousseuses		S	M			H		
Goethe	H	H						
Gracilis	S	S				S		
Henri Martin								
Jeanne de Montfort	H							
Julie de Mersan	H	M						
Laneii	S			M		S		
Louis Gimard	M							
Mme. de la Rôche-Lambert	M	S				M		
Mme. Louis Lévêque	S		S	M		S		
Mossman	M	S				M		
Nuits de Young					S ·	S		
OEillet Panacheé					S	S		
Perpetual White Moss					S	M		
Robert Léopold		S			S	M		
Salet			M	S		S		
Violacée						S		
Waldtraut Nielsen		S						
White Bath				S				
William Lobb								
SHRUB ROSES								
A. MacKenzie	—		—	M	—		—	
Adelaide Hoodless	M	H	M	M		H		S
Alchymist		S	S	S		S		
Amiga Mia	—	S	—	M	—		—	
Applejack								
Blue Boy		—		—		—		—
Bonica		S						
Carefree Beauty						S		
Chamcook	S					S		
Champlain			S	S				
Country Dancer	—	S	—		—		—	
Golden Wings		S						
Haidee					S	S		
J. P. Connell	—	M	—		—		—	
John Franklin		S				S		S
Lillian Gibson						S		S
Morden Amorette	S	H	S			M		
Morden Cardinette	—	H	—		—		—	
Morden Centennial	S	M						M
Morden Ruby	—	H	—		—		—	
Prairie Dawn	M	M			M	M		
Prairie Princess	—	S	—		—		—	
Prairie Wren			S		S			
Prairie Youth	H	M			S	M	M	
Robusta	—	M	—		—		—	

CULTIVAR	BLACKSPOT		POWDERY MILDEW		LEAF SPOTS		RUST	
	1990	1992	1990	1992	1990	1992	1990	1992
Scharlachglut						M	S	M
Summer Wind								
Von Scharnhorst	S					S		
SPECIES								
Dr. Merkeley	M				S	S		M
R. ambylotis			S		S	S		
R. arkansana			H					
R. canina	H		S			S		M
R. cinnamomea	S					S		M
R. foetida	H	H				S		
R. foetida bicolor	H	—		—		—		—
R. glauca	H				S	M		
R. hugonis				S		S		
R. laxa	S		S			S		
R. macounii	S		M	S		M		M
R. mollis	S					S		
R. multiflora						S		
R. nitida	M		M	M	S	S		
R. palustris		S	S	M		S		
R. pendulina	M					M	M	
R. pomifera	S	S	S	S	S	S		
R. primula								
R. rugosa								S
R. rugosa alba plena								
R. rugosa kamtchatica			H		S	S		
R. sertata			M		S	M		
R. setigera						S		
R. spinosissima altaica								
R. virginiana			M	M	M	S		
R. woodsii	H		S			M		

Insects

Roses are hosts to many insect pests. Aphids, mites, rose stem borers, and gall wasps were the four most common insect pests observed between 1989 and 1992 at the Minnesota Landscape Arboretum. Leaf miners, leafhoppers, thrips, and other chewing and skeletonizing insects were seen occasionally.

Aphids

These small insects are one of the more common pests of roses. They are soft-bodied, usually lime green, and are found on cane tips, flower buds, and on the bottom of new leaves, where they puncture the plant to suck juices. As they feed, they excrete a sticky and glossy residue called "honeydew." Severe infestations can lead to drying and curling of new leaves. Pesticides and natural predators, such as ladybugs, provide control for aphid infestations.

Figure 10. Aphids feeding on Rosa *'Robusta'. The larval stage of ladybugs, called "lions," are feeding on the aphids.*

Mites

Mites are also common on roses, but are difficult to see because of their very small size. They pierce foliage and suck plant sap from leaves. The yellowing and mottling of leaves that result are often the first symp-

Stippling caused by mites.

toms observed. Mites also form fine webs on the undersides of leaves where they feed. Severe infestation causes defoliation. Mites are most often seen under dry conditions.

Cultural practices that result in vigorously growing roses are a gardener's best defense against mites. Pesticides are commonly used to eliminate severe infestations. Dormant oil, which smothers mite eggs, is often applied to dormant bushes. Natural predators of mites can also be purchased for biological control. Repeated water sprays of infested plants, especially at the undersides of leaves, will help control but not eliminate mites.

Rose Stem Borer

The rose stem borer, *Agrilus aurichalceus*, damages rose canes when larvae tunnel in a spiral fashion beneath the bark, girdling and killing the canes (figures below). Their presence is indicated when a cane dies above the point of borer tunneling. Leaves on the infected cane turn brown as they die, creating a "flag" among healthy, green-leaved canes. On close observation, a swelling or gall on the infected cane can be seen below the dead tissue, indicating where the borer's tunneling occurred. The gall formation weakens canes and it is common to see infected canes broken off by wind. The quickest and most effective control is removal and disposal of infected canes in fall.

From left to right: rose stem borer flag, rose stem borer gall, and rose stem borer tunneling.

Mossy Rose Gall

Mossy rose galls are caused by *Diplolepis spinosa*, a cynipid gall wasp. These galls are common on wild roses of North America, from Ontario to Alberta in Canada and throughout most of the northern United States. They are becoming common on Rugosa cultivars.[17] The presence of these insects is indicated by the formation of spherical, golf ball-size, spiny galls on the canes of host plants.

The development of these galls is stimulated in the spring by newly hatched larvae. The galls encase the larvae until adult wasps emerge the following spring. The galls are unsightly and alter the plant's shape. They also stress the host plant, behaving like nutrient sinks, drawing nutrients away from the rest of the plant.[17, 18] Large numbers of galls on a plant can kill the plant.

Mossy rose galls caused by Diplolepis spinosa *on rose canes. Hybrid Rugosas are particularly susceptible to this disfiguring gall.*

Insecticides have no effect on the wasp that causes mossy rose gall. The most effective control is physical removal and disposal of galls in autumn after leaves have dropped and galls are visible. It is important to dispose of all galls since even a single missed gall can produce and reintroduce 30 to 40 mature wasps to the garden the following spring.

Insect Observations

Observations of aphid, mite, mossy rose gall, and rose stem borer occurrence in the Arboretum's Shrub Rose Garden from 1989 through 1992 are provided in Table 9. Insect pest occurrence was highest among Hybrid Rugosa cultivars, with cultivars among other classifications infected less often. Sixty-eight percent of the insect pest observations occurred on Hybrid Rugosa cultivars or on *R. rugosa* species.

[17] J.D. Shorthouse. Cynipid Galls of Shrub Roses. *The American Rose Magazine*, May 1993. pp 16-17.

[18] G. Bagatto, T.J. Zmijowskyj, and J.D. Shorthouse. Galls Induced by *Diplolepis spinosa* Influence Distribution of Mineral Nutrients in the Shrub Rose. *HortScience* 26(10): 1283-1284. 1991.

Although aphids and mites often favor particular cultivars when feeding on roses, they commonly feed across all classes of roses. In contrast, mossy rose galls caused by *Diplolepis spinosa* were seen only on Hybrid Rugosa cultivars and Species Roses.

Rose stem borer damage occurred primarily on Hybrid Rugosa cultivars and *R. rugosa* species. The occurrence of the rose stem borer was, however, more widespread than this evaluation shows. Because the borer was not diagnosed until late in the study, early observations of borer symptoms were pooled with other unexplained symptoms.

Although the occurrence of the rose stem borer was highest among Hybrid Rugosa cultivars, they were also found on cultivars in other rose classes. They have been observed on 'Lillian Gibson', 'Prairie Dawn', and 'Alba semi-plena' since the end of the evaluation.

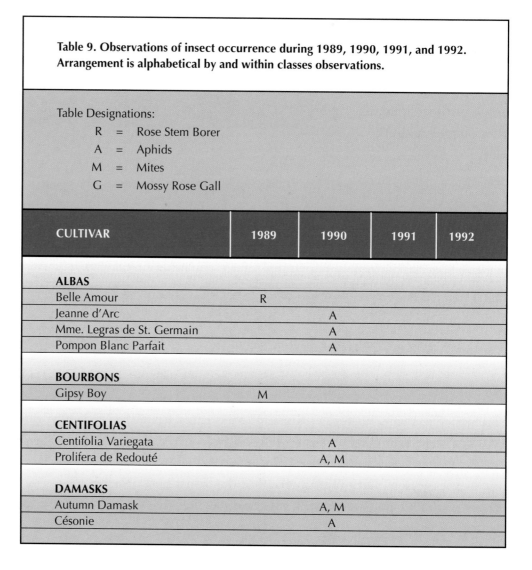

Table 9. Observations of insect occurrence during 1989, 1990, 1991, and 1992. Arrangement is alphabetical by and within classes observations.

Table Designations:

R	=	Rose Stem Borer
A	=	Aphids
M	=	Mites
G	=	Mossy Rose Gall

CULTIVAR	1989	1990	1991	1992
ALBAS				
Belle Amour	R			
Jeanne d'Arc		A		
Mme. Legras de St. Germain		A		
Pompon Blanc Parfait		A		
BOURBONS				
Gipsy Boy	M			
CENTIFOLIAS				
Centifolia Variegata		A		
Prolifera de Redouté		A, M		
DAMASKS				
Autumn Damask		A, M		
Césonie		A		

CULTIVAR	1989	1990	1991	1992
Léda		A		
Marie Louise		M		
GALLICAS				
Alice Vena				A
Belle Isis		M		
HYBRID NITIDAS				
Metis				R
HYBRID PERPETUALS				
Mme. Scipion Cochet				A
Mrs. John Laing				A
HYBRID RUGOSAS				
Agnes				A, G
Amelia Gravereaux		A, G		A, G
Belle Poitevine		A	G	G
Blanc Double de Coubert	G		G	R
Bonavista				M
Delicata	G			
Elmira		M		M
Frau Dagmar Hartopp	G	A, M	G	M
George Will				G
Grootendorst Supreme	G, M	M	G	
Hansa	G, M	G	G	G
Henry Hudson	M	M		R, M
Hunter	G	A		A, G
Martin Frobisher	M			
Moncton		M		
Mrs. John McNabb		G	G	G
Pink Grootendorst	M	M		A, R
Rugosa Magnifica		M	G	
Sir Thomas Lipton	G	A		A
Thérèse Bauer	G, M	A	G	
Thérèse Bugnet	G		G	
Will Alderman	M			R
HYBRID SUFFULTAS				
Assiniboine				M
MOSSES				
Black Boy		R		
Gloire des Mousseuses		M		
OEillet Panacheé	M			
Perpetual White Moss				A
Salet	M			
SHRUB ROSES				
Adelaide Hoodless		M		M

CULTIVAR	1989	1990	1991	1992
Alchymist				A
Champlain	M			
Golden Wings				A
Lillian Gibson			M	M
SPECIES				
R. multiflora				M
R. pomifera		M		
R. rugosa				G
R. rugosa alba plena				M, R
R. sertata			G	G

The Hybrid Rugosa 'Frau Dagmar Hartopp' has large, single, light pink, fragrant blossoms. Flowers and large red hips appear together in late summer and fall.

Cultivation Tips

Site Selection

A site that provides full sunlight, good air circulation, and a well-drained soil high in organic matter is ideal for rose growing. Roses receiving fewer than six hours of sun daily will be leggy, less floriferous, and more disease-prone. The number of roses that grow and perform well in partial shade is small. If roses are crowded by neighboring plants or buildings, air movement is restricted and disease incidence increases.

Water movement through the soil should be slow enough to allow water and nutrients to be absorbed by roots. But excess water must be able to drain away quickly, because rose growth and performance deteriorate rapidly if roots are waterlogged. If an 18-inch hole filled with water drains in six to eight hours, drainage is satisfactory. Soil that drains more quickly is sandy and can be improved by the addition of organic matter such as composted plant materials, peat moss, or composted manure. Adding organic matter will improve the texture and drainage of compacted or clay soils that drain too slowly.

When soil drainage problems cannot be corrected, raised beds can also be used for growing roses. Construction materials for the beds must be carefully selected because creosote or copper-treated timbers are toxic to roses.

Checking soil pH and nutrition prior to planting is important. A soil pH of 6.0 - 7.0 optimizes nutrient uptake in roses. Nitrogen moves easily through the soil and can be applied before or after planting. Phosphorous and potassium do not move easily or far in soil, so it is more effective to incorporate them prior to planting. County extension agents can refer gardeners to laboratories that can analyze soil samples and recommend amendments to optimize fertility and pH for a rose garden.

Garden size depends on the number of roses being planted, their mature sizes, and on spacing between plants. Remember that good air flow around roses results in healthier plants, and space your plants accordingly. Because of rose thorns, it is also important to leave enough space between plants to ensure that maintenance can be done as painlessly as possible.

Purchasing Plants

Local nurseries usually sell roses as container-grown plants that are actively growing and sometimes blooming, so gardeners can see what plants looks like before purchasing them. Container-grown plants can be planted any time through the growing season. Because of the additional care and handling involved in potting and forcing a bareroot plant into growth at the nursery, container-grown roses are more expensive than bareroot roses.

Mail order companies provide a more extensive choice of roses. Most are shipped dormant, with bare roots wrapped in a moisture-retaining material. The time of year that mail order sources ship roses depends on where you live. In Minnesota, expect shipment in early to mid-May.

The *Combined Rose List*[19] and the *Andersen Horticultural Library's Source List of Plants and Seeds*[20] are international and national listings, respectively, of retail sources for particular rose cultivars.

Most roses are propagated by budding, which is the placement of a bud from one cultivar onto a rootstock of another. Rootstocks are usually thornless selections of the species *R. multiflora, R. canina,* or *R. Laxa.* The bud union, the site where the cultivar and rootstock are joined, is a distinctively swollen area on the shank (see figure on page 75). All basal canes of the cultivar emerge from the bud union. The rootstock used in budding often furnishes the plant with extreme vigor. For the gardener, this means that a plant may have a larger mature size than it would if it were on its own roots. For the rose propagator, it means that sizable plants can be produced quickly, consistently, and economically.

The rootstock of a budded rose will often send up suckers with flowers and leaves completely different from the variety budded onto it. Removal of these suckers can be a constant chore for gardeners.

Incompatability between a rootstock and the budded variety can occur. When this occurs, the vigor and quality of the budded cultivar declines over time, until finally the cultivar dies, leaving only the rootstock to send up new canes.

In northern climates, low winter temperatures can injure the bud union and cultivar growing above the union. Planting the rose with the bud union below ground for insulation is the best way to ensure bud

[19] B.R. Dobson, *Combined Rose List,* B.R. Dobson (pub), Irvington, NY. Annual.

[20] R.T. Isaacson, *Andersen Horticultural Library's Source List of Plants and Seeds,* Andersen Horticultural Library, Chanhassen, Minnesota. 1993.

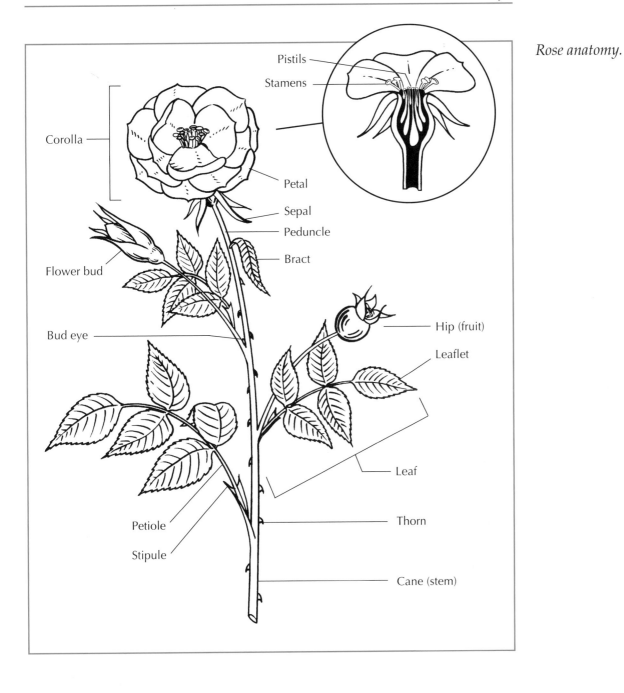

Rose anatomy.

Pistils

Stamens

Corolla

Petal

Sepal

Peduncle

Bract

Flower bud

Hip (fruit)

Leaflet

Bud eye

Leaf

Thorn

Petiole

Stipule

Cane (stem)

union survival, so that new canes produced in the spring are from the cultivar rather than the rootstock.

Because of consumer demand, especially among northern gardeners, own-root roses produced by softwood propagation are becoming more available. These roses are produced by inducing roots to form on stem cuttings. With own-root roses, the chore of removing rootstock suckers disappears. Plants growing on their own roots are also often long-lived in comparison to budded plants. Since the root system is genetically identical to the canes, the gardener is assured that new basal canes produced each year are true to the cultivar.

Newly purchased budded roses vary in size. All plants should have a well developed root system, but the number, length, and diameter of canes will vary with grade (1, 1$\frac{1}{2}$, or 2). Grade 1 roses are the highest quality and the most expensive. They have three or more canes growing from the bud union for most rose classes. Grade 2 roses have the fewest, shortest, or thinnest canes.

A cultivar budded and grown in a warmer climate is often larger than the same cultivar budded and grown in a cooler climate. The plants are genetically identical, but there are size differences due to the effect of climate and other growing conditions on growth rate. Bigger is also not always better, since larger plants are more susceptible to transplant shock.

Newly purchased softwood-propagated roses also vary in size, ranging from small, 6-inch, potted plants that need additional care and container growth before being planted, to bareroot, 3-foot plants.

After receiving a rose, whether potted or bareroot, it is essential to keep the roots moist. Potted roses that cannot be planted immediately should be placed in a warm spot out of the wind, and soil moisture should be checked daily. If receiving a dormant bareroot rose, open the package as soon as possible. If you can plant immediately, immerse the rose in a bucket of water for at least a few hours before planting to rehydrate the plant. If you cannot plant immediately, check to see that the roots and the moisture-retaining material around them are still moist, wrap the rose back up in its plastic covering, store it in a dark, cool spot, and check the plant's moisture level daily. If the ground is not frozen, bareroot roses that will not be planted within two weeks of shipment should be temporarily heeled in. Dig a trench or hole in the ground, lay the rose in it, and cover the roots and canes with moist soil.

Planting

Potted roses can be planted at any time during the growing season, but the earlier the plant is put into the ground, the more time it has to establish before the onset of winter. Bareroot plants should be planted in early spring while they are still dormant. Unless very heavy mulch is applied, fall planting of roses is not recommended in northern areas because soil temperatures drop too quickly to allow root establishment.

Planting on a calm, cloudy day avoids desiccation of roots and canes. Begin by digging a hole twice as wide as the root ball diameter.

If organic matter needs to be incorporated, mix compost, composted manure, or peat moss with the soil from the hole. Incorporating bonemeal into the soil at this time provides a long-term source of phosphorous and promotes rooting.

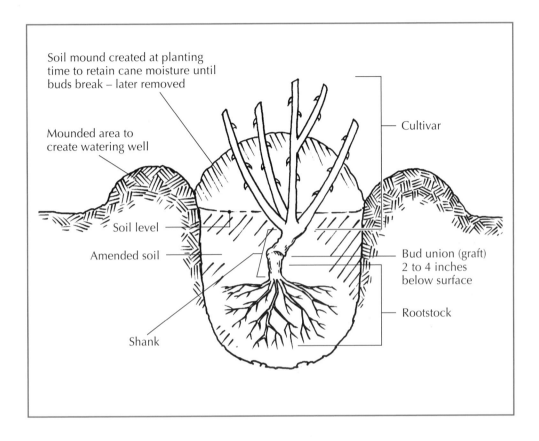

Soil mound created at planting time to retain cane moisture until buds break – later removed

Mounded area to create watering well

Cultivar

Soil level

Amended soil

Bud union (graft) 2 to 4 inches below surface

Rootstock

Shank

Minimize root disturbance when planting a potted rose. If possible, cut the bottom of the container out, place the pot in the planting hole, slit the side of the pot, and remove it. If the roots are a dense mass circling the perimeter of the root ball, shallow cuts should be made in several places down the side of the root ball. This encourages new root growth out into the surrounding soil.

On bareroot roses, any broken canes or roots should be trimmed away. If roots are excessively long, shorten them rather than twisting them around the bottom of the planting hole. Prune the canes back to a height of 6 to 8 inches. This encourages basal bud breaks and creates a stronger, bushier plant.

If the plant was propagated by budding, place the plant in the hole with the bud union 2 to 4 inches below ground level. This insulates and protects the bud union. Plant an own-root rose at the same depth at which it was previously growing.

Hardiness Zones: The winter hardiness evaluation reported in this bulletin was conducted in Zone 4a, where average annual minimum temperatures ranges from –25° to –30°F (–32° to –34°C).

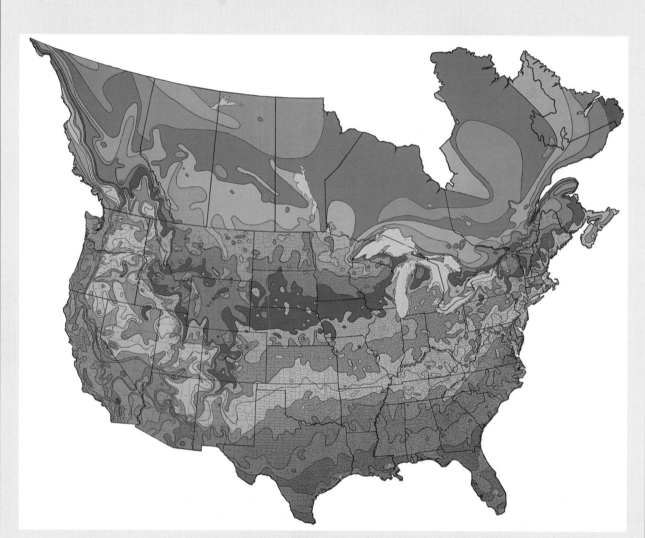

Average Annual Minimum Temperatures for Hardiness Zones

CELSIUS	Zone	FAHRENHEIT					
			–28.9 to –31.6	4b	–20 to –25	–9.5 to –12.2	8a	15 to 10
–45.6 and Below	1	Below –50	–26.2 to –28.8	5a	–15 to –20	–6.7 to –9.4	8b	20 to 15
–42.8 to –45.5	2a	–45 to –50	–23.4 to –26.1	5b	–10 to –15	–3.9 to –6.6	9a	25 to 20
–40.0 to –42.7	2b	–40 to –45	–20.6 to –23.3	6a	–5 to –10	–1.2 to –3.8	9b	30 to 25
–37.3 to –40.0	3a	–35 to –40	–17.8 to –20.5	6b	0 to –5	1.6 to –1.1	10a	35 to 30
–34.5 to –37.2	3b	–30 to –35	–15.0 to –17.7	7a	5 to 0	4.4 to 1.7	10b	40 to 35
–31.7 to –34.4	4a	–25 to –30	–12.3 to –15.0	7b	10 to 5	4.5 and Above	11	40 and Above

Put half of the soil back into the hole around the roots, tamp it lightly to eliminate air pockets, and add the remainder of the soil. Construct a rim of soil around the planting hole to create a shallow well, and water the plant thoroughly by filling the well.

Mound 6 to 8 inches of soil up around newly planted dormant rose bushes. Keep this mound moist so that the canes and buds within remain moist until the buds break, typically within about 14 days. When buds start to expand, gently wash the mound of soil away, preferably on a cloudy day.

Water, Mulch, and Fertilizer

The common rule for rose irrigation is 1 inch of water per week during the growing season. This is especially important during the first growing season of a newly planted rose.

The amount of water needed by established roses depends on the soil it is planted in. Roses in sandy soils will need more water than those in heavier soils. Excessively hot temperatures for extended periods call for more frequent watering. Mulched beds retain soil moisture longer than unmulched beds.

A slow, soaking application of water which penetrates 15 to 18 inches into the ground is best. Wetting the foliage of roses during irrigation should be avoided to discourage disease development.

Mulches help retain soil moisture, moderate soil tempertures, decrease erosion, and discourage weeds. Organic mulches such as wood chips, straw, and grass clippings will improve soil quality as they break down. However, large amounts of nitrogen can be bound up as an organic mulch decomposes, often at the expense of the roses, so additional applications of nitrogen may be needed. Organic mulches that decompose need to be reapplied regularly.

Fertilization programs should vary depending on rose type. One application of a balanced fertilizer in early spring is adequate for Species Roses. All other roses will benefit from a second application at the end of the spring bloom period. A third application in late July helps repeat-flowering and continually blooming roses. Fertilization after August 1 is not recommended, because this encourages new growth and delays cold hardening.

Deadheading

Deadheading is the removal of spent flowers from a rose bush so that hips, the rose fruit, do not form. This maximizes rebloom on repeat-flowering roses by diverting the energy normally used for hip development into new flowers and cane growth. If a rose is female-sterile, deadheading occurs naturally as spent flowers drop off the plant.

The only reasons for deadheading a one-time-blooming rose are to give the plant a cleaner appearance or to maximize vegetative growth. Not deadheading these roses or any rose whose rebloom is less than showy allows gardeners to take advantage of the ornamental value of fall hip display.

Methods for deadheading should vary between types of roses. For instance, the usual method of deadheading Hybrid Teas and Floribundas is to remove a spent flower and the cane beneath it back to the first outward-facing leaf with five leaflets. Deadheading back to a leaf with fewer leaflets often results in non-flowering new growth, called "blind wood."

The location of new shoot and new flower formation is more variable among hardy repeat-flowering roses. New flowering wood can be produced from a bud at the bract beneath a flower or from buds at any leaf axis. On these roses, it is better to deadhead back to the bract beneath the flower, and observe whether new flowering wood grows from this point. If flowers are not produced, prune back to the first leaf and start the observation process again. Continue deadheading back to the highest leaf on a cane until you know the pattern or growth and bloom for a cultivar.

Do not deadhead after September 1. This allows hips to form, which signals the plant to slow its growth and go dormant in preparation for winter.

Pruning and Winter Protection

There are several reasons to prune a Shrub Rose besides deadheading to maximize rebloom. Pruning a newly planted rose to a height of 6 to 8 inches minimizes transplant shock, making the establishment process easier for the plant. It also encourages bud break at the base of the plant, producing fewer and stronger canes and a denser form.

In northern climates, winter injury to canes can be severe. Pruning to remove this injured wood is done in the spring. As roses age, it is often necessary to remove old canes that have become less vigorous and less floriferous. Removing these canes opens the center of the plant, encourages new cane formation, and improves air circulation. One-third of the canes can be removed annually without hurting the plant.

Removing weak, spindly growth from a rose allows it to divert its energy to stronger, more vigorous canes. This improves the health of the whole plant. Pruning is also done to alter and improve plant habit or size.

Providing winter protection for a newly planted rose will improve its chance of surviving the first winter, before it has completely established. After roses are established, a gardener's choice of the level of winter protection to be provided should be guided by two factors: the hardiness of the cultivar and the level of cane injury acceptable to the gardener. Local nursery operators and rosarians may be able to provide information on a rose's hardiness level during a typical winter in your area. Because descriptive text on a new cultivar may also list the rose as hardy to a particular temperature or hardiness zone, North American plant hardiness zone maps, such as the one on page 76, can also be a valuable aid in selecting appropriate cultivars. Individual gardeners then have to decide how much cane injury is tolerable, and protect roses accordingly.

Snowcover, when present, is a natural insulator of rose canes. Tipping and covering, soil mounding, wood chips, and leaves enclosed with chicken wire are ways to provide winter protection.

Pest Control

Recommendations for controlling diseases and insects with chemical pesticides change constantly as old products are removed from the market and new ones become available.

The best way to keep abreast of current pest control recommendations is to obtain the most current university extension publications[21] or to contact local county extension agents. Consulting Rosarians in rose societies can also often recommend control programs.

---

[21] The Minnesota Extension Service "Rose Diseases" fact sheet is an example. The 1995 revision is included in the Appendix.

Monthly averages for maximum and minimum air temperatures and monthly precipitation for 1990 (top) and 1992 (bottom).*

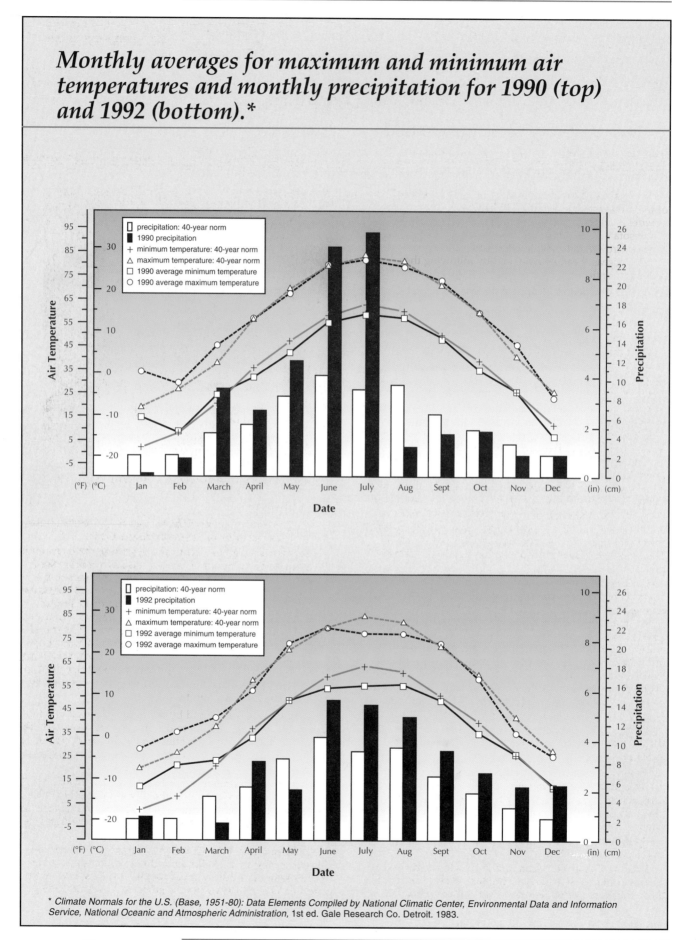

* Climate Normals for the U.S. (Base, 1951-80): Data Elements Compiled by National Climatic Center, Environmental Data and Information Service, National Oceanic and Atmospheric Administration, 1st ed. Gale Research Co. Detroit. 1983.

FS-1163-A
Revised 1995

MINNESOTA EXTENSION SERVICE

UNIVERSITY OF MINNESOTA
COLLEGE OF AGRICULTURAL, FOOD,
AND ENVIRONMENTAL SCIENCES

Rose Diseases

F.L. Pfleger and S.L. Gould

Roses are vulnerable to many diseases. Fortunately, few of these diseases are common in Minnesota. Black spot, powdery mildew, and Botrytis blight may afflict Minnesota's roses. Other diseases in the state are rust, cankers, crown gall, wilt, and viruses.

Such diseases can be managed by following these recommendations:

- Buy certified stock free of disease;
- Keep plants free of weeds, fallen leaves, and disease-infested plants or canes;
- Use spray programs and cultural methods suggested in this fact sheet.

Black Spot is caused by the fungus *Diplocarpon rosae.* The disease can cause almost complete defoliation of bushes by early fall. It produces a weakened bush on which cane dieback, stem canker, and winter injury can become severe.

Symptoms: Circular black spots ranging from 1/16 inch to 1/2 inch in diameter appear generally on leaves' upper sides. The spots are frequently surrounded by a yellow halo. Infected leaves characteristically turn yellow. They fall prematurely. This leaf spot can be distinguished from others by the fringed margin and consistently black color. Cane infection produces a reddish-purple spot. In many varieties, pale flower color is also indirectly caused.

Disease Cycle: Black spot is spread by splashing water. Infection occurs after leaves are wet for several hours. Therefore, the disease is more serious during periods of rainfall.

Control: A preventive program for black spot should begin with a thorough clean-up in the fall. Diseased leaves on the ground should be raked and destroyed. All diseased canes should be pruned off by cutting several inches into good wood. These precautions reduce overwintering fungi.

A fungicide program should start in the summer just before leaves become spotted. From then until frost, the leaves may require a protective fungicide coating. When the leaves are growing rapidly or during rainy weather, it may be necessary to spray the plants two times a week. However, if growth is less rapid and rains are less frequent, spraying at 7-10 day intervals is usually sufficient. Proper timing is as important as the chemical spray. A preventive spray program can include the chemicals listed in table 1.

Powdery Mildew is caused by the fungus *Sphaerotheca pannosa.* This disease can cause young leaves to curl and turn purple. Young canes may be distorted and dwarfed. If seriously infected, they can die. Badly infected buds do not open.

Symptoms: Leaves, buds, and stems are covered with a white powdery coating.

Disease Cycle: The white fuzzy growth on the leaf surface contains thousands of fungus spores. Wind carries these spores to young leaves, causing more infection.

Figure 1. Black spot.

Mildew diseases of other plants do not infect roses. Mildew develops rapidly during warm, humid weather.

Control: Throughout the growing season, the infection can be reduced through sanitation and fungicide application. Pruning and destroying all dead or diseased canes in the spring will reduce the initial fungus population. During the growing season, all diseased leaves should be destroyed. New growth is especially susceptible. Therefore, a thorough spray or dust coverage of canes and upper and lower leaf surfaces (especially growing tips) is essential. Under most conditions, weekly applications are adequate. However, treat more often during rapid new growth, temperature fluctuations, and frequent rains. A preventive spray program can include chemicals listed in table 1.

Botrytis Blight is caused by the fungus *Botrytis cinerea.* The disease causes flower buds to droop and remain closed. Buds turn brown and decay. Sometimes partially opened buds are attacked, and an entire flower may be covered by gray fungus.

Symptoms: A smooth, slightly sunken, grayish-black lesion may develop just below the flower head. The bud is destroyed. It frequently hangs over at or near the lesion. The fungus may also infect stub ends of stems from which flowers have been cut.

Disease Cycle: Botrytis is a gray fungus that generally lives on dying tissue. With the right conditions, any dead plant tissue can release thousands of botrytis spores. Botrytis infection occurs when water remains on leaves or buds.

Figure 2. Powdery mildew.

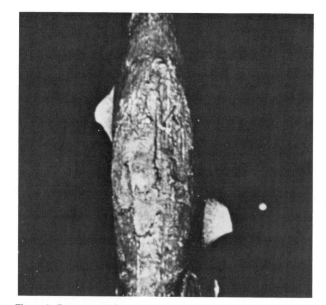

Figure 3. Rose stem infected with brown canker fungus. Note the dark swollen area on the cane, characteristic of this disease.

Control: Cut and destroy all infected blossoms as soon as they droop or die. To prevent large numbers of fungus spores, clean dead plant material on which spores are produced. Fungicide application may be necessary. A preventive spray program can include chemicals listed in table 1.

Brown Canker is caused by the fungus *Cryptosporella umbrina*. The disease is commonly found on outdoor roses and occasionally on greenhouse-grown roses. The fungus is capable of attacking any portion of the plant above ground and can result in death of the entire stem.

Symptoms: Small red to purple spots appear on the current year's canes and with time, these spots usually develop into gray-white lesions on the stem surface. A whitish patch can be seen as the small spots are massed together. Often times little damage occurs the first year, however, in time the white lesions continue to enlarge and brown cankers (several inches long) form girdling the stem resulting in death (figure 3). The cankers may extend down into the crown of the plant and may destroy the entire plant.

Disease Cycle: The fungus overwinters in infected canes and spores can be spread to healthy canes by splashing water, wind, and pruning tools. However, the pathogen can only enter plant tissue through wounds.

Control: If a new rose planting is to be established, care should be taken to select disease-free planting stock to prevent the introduction of brown canker. In established rose plantings, all dead and dying canes should be pruned out and destroyed. In removing diseased canes, make cuts well below the diseased areas. Before each cut is made it is advisable to dip the pruning shears in a 1:10 chlorine bleach: water dilution. Since this pathogen enters the stem through wounds, care should be taken to avoid stem injury.

Table 1.

Chemical	Formulated products	Disease				
		Black spot	Botrytis	Powdery Mildew	Rust	Brown Canker
Captan	Captan 50% WP; Rose and Floral Dust; Orthocide	+	+	+		
Chlorothalonil	Daconil 2787; Fungicide with Daconil; Multi-purpose Fungicide	+	+	+	+	
Copper	Bordeaux; Copper Fungicide; Phyton 27	+	+	+	+	
Lime-Sulfur	Dormant Disease Control; Lime-Sulfur Spray	+		+	+	
Mancozeb	Mancozeb Flowable with Zinc; Cleary's Protect T/O	+	+			
Sulfur	Garden Sulfur; Rose, Floral, and Vegetable Dust; Wettable Dusting Sulphur	+		+		+
Triforine	Triforine EC; Funginex; Orthenex	+		+	+	

For small jobs, it is often necessary to determine the amount of pesticide required in one gallon of spray. When the recommended rate is in lbs./100 gal., use the following conversion for a one gallon spray mix.
A) Wettable powders
 1 level Tbls./1 gal. of water is approximately 1 lb./100 gal.
B) Emulsions
 1 tsp./1 gal. of water is approximately 1 pt./100 gal.

This information is current as of the date this was printed. Read and follow the label directions for the use of all pesticides.

F.L. Pfleger, *professor*
S.L. Gould, *assistant scientist*
Plant Pathology

Produced by the Educational Development System, Minnesota Extension Service.

The information given in this publication is for educational purposes only. Reference to commercial products or trade names is made with the understanding that no discrimination is intended and no endorsement by the Minnesota Extension Service is implied.

This material is available in alternative formats upon request. Please contact your Minnesota County Extension Office, or, outside of Minnesota, contact the Distribution Center at (612) 625-8173.

The University, including the Minnesota Extension Service, is an equal opportunity educator and employer.   Recycled paper, 10% postconsumer waste.

The following text and table were originally published in 1975 in the University of Minnesota's Agricultural Extension Service publication *Arboretum Review* (No. 22-1975). It has been out of print for many years, but contains hardiness observations on many cultivars no longer grown at the Minnesota Landscape Arboretum and therefore not included in the study on which this publication is based. The American Rose Society now assigns many of these cultivars to different classes than they were considered to be in at the time of the original publication.

Shrub and Old-fashioned Roses

Leon C. Snyder

There is a growing interest in roses that do not require complete winter protection. To find out which shrub and species roses can be grown in Minnesota, the arboretum has planted several hundred different species and cultivars in a special planting area The old-fashioned roses are sponsored by the Kenwood Garden Club. The modern shrub and species roses are sponsored by the Minnesota Rose Society. Distinction between modern and old-fashioned roses is arbitrary. Any variety that was developed and introduced at least 100 years ago is considered old-fashioned.

The old-fashioned and modern shrub roses will be considered under these classes:

> Albas
> Bourbons
> Centifolias
> Damasks
> Gallicas
> Hybrid Musks
> Hybrid Perpetuals
> Modern Shrub Roses
> Moss
> Rugosa Hybrids
> Species

These groups differ in breeding and time of introduction. Some bloom just once during the season, while others have repeat bloom. Some develop colorful hips or fruits in late summer and fall.

Alba roses are thought to have originated in the Crimea from a natural hybrid between *Rosa damascena* and a white form of the Dog Rose (*Rosa canina*). Alba roses gained their greatest popularity in England where they were introduced by the earliest Roman

traders before 77 A.D. At the peak of their popularity in England during the last century, over 100 cultivars were listed. Today only about 20 cultivars are in the trade. Ten of these have been tested in the arboretum. These cultivars all flower in June and range from single to fully double. The flowers are very fragrant. Winter injury can vary from none to severe, depending on the cultivar and the severity of the winter.

Bourbon roses are of relatively recent origin. They originated in the Indian Ocean on the island known as L'Isle Bourbon (Reunion). Soon after the introduction of the China Rose (*Rosa chinensis*) to the west, plants of this species were planted as hedges on the island's farms. It was the custom to plant a hedge of the Pink China rose on one side of the property and a hedge of the Autumn Damask on the other. A.M. Perichon discovered one rose differed markedly from either species. He took it to his garden, and when it bloomed, it was evident the rose was a natural hybrid. In 1822, M. Breon, a plant scout for the French government, visited the island. He saw this new rose and sent plants and seeds to

Paris. From plantings in Paris, several cultivars were selected and named. Hybridization between the China and Damask roses continued. Those that bloomed only in the spring were put into a class called Hybrid Chinas. Those that had repeat blooms were called Bourbons. Of the hundreds of Bourbons that were listed by writers, only a few are left. Eleven have been

tested in our trials. Generally, the plants are similar to the Hybrid Teas in their flowers. Winter injury can vary from none to severe, depending on the winter and the cultivar.

Centifolia roses developed in about 1700 after about a century of breeding by Dutch nurserymen. Cytological studies indicate that *Rosa damascena* and *Rosa alba* were involved in the ancestry. This class shows similarities between the two species. The flowers are white to deep pink. The plants are taller than the Damask roses and have more pronounced prickles. We have tested 11 of these Centifolias. These have been quite hardy, with good bloom in June.

Damask roses had an early origin; they were known in early Greek times. Two types exist: the Summer Damask; and the Autumn Damask. For both types, the female parent was *Rosa gallica*. The male parent is a matter of conjecture. For the Summer Damask *(Rosa x damascena)*, the male parent is probably *Rosa phoenicia*. For the Autumn Damask *(Rosa x damascena bifera)*, the male parent is probably *Rosa moschata*. The Summer Damask roses are quite upright with stems that have prickles mixed with strong, hooked thorns. Foliage is grayish green, covered with hairs. Blooms are pink to white, semidouble to very double and fragrant. Autumn Damask roses are becoming quite rare. The plant habit is similar to the

Summer Damask, but the foliage is olive-green. The fruits are elongated and funnel-form as contrasted to the round fruits of the Summer Damask. These roses have been quite hardy.

Gallica roses are of ancient origin. The Apothecary's Rose, *Rosa gallica off officinalis*, was cultivated at the time of the Roman Empire; it was, no doubt, brought to England and France by the Romans. In the 13th century, a sizeable industry developed in the town of Provins, France, based on the use of the rose petals in a conserve that was supposed to cure many ailments. The variety *officinalis* was brought to America by early colonists and was widely planted. The striped variety, versi-color, called 'Rosa Mundi,' is apparently a sport of *officinalis*. The number of its cultivars increased rapidly during the 17th century, with thousands listed by 1800. These cultivars were similar, being difficult to distinguish. Fortunately, the number of cultivars has declined; now only a few are available. We have about 20 in our collection.

Most of the Gallicas have branches that are erect and stiff. They are seldom more than 5 to 6 feet tall. The prickles are weak, straight, and rather sparse. The leaves have five leaflets and are thick and rough. Blooms are pink to red and include single, semidouble, and double types. Individual flowers are borne on stiff, erect stems. Most Gallicas have proven to be quite hardy.

Hybrid Musk roses are of comparatively recent origin, having originated early in this century from crosses made by Reverend J.R. Pemberton of England. Most of the cultivars resulted from crosses between *Rosa multiflora* and the Noisette roses that were developed from the Musk rose, *Rosa moschata*, crossed with the China rose, *Rosa chinensis*, or one of its hybrids. The Hybrid Musk roses resemble *R. multiflora* more than they do *R. moschata*. They are vigorous, pillar-type roses that exhibit repeat bloom. The flowers vary greatly in size, and they range from single to fully double. As a group, they lack winter hardiness, usually freezing back to the snow or ground line. They usually sprout from the base, and once the dead wood is removed, they develop into attractive plants with good fall bloom. Although we grow ours without support, they would be more attractive if trained on pillars or a trellis. A mulch applied around the base of the plants is advised for winter protection.

Hybrid Perpetuals appeared in the middle of the 19th century. The exact origin is not clear, and, no doubt, numerous species and cultivars were involved. Undoubtedly, the Gallica and China roses entered into the early breeding. The bloom is certainly not continuous or perpetual, but most varieties do form a few flowers on new wood. The greatest display, however, comes in June. The flowers are mostly double, fragrant, and some shade of pink. Interest in the Hybrid Perpetuals has declined since the introduction of the Hybrid Teas. Most varieties have a fair degree of hardiness, but die back is common. A winter mulch is advised.

Moss roses are special in the rose world. The early mosses developed as sports of the Centifolias. They differ by having green, mosslike growth on the sepals. Later, cultivars of moss roses have been developed by hybridization with other species and cultivars. The moss roses were developed largely in the last century, but roses with the moss characteristic are still being developed. Most true moss roses bloom once—in late June, although some more recent hybrids have repeat bloom in June. Some die back can be expected most years.

Rugosa Hybrids. The Rugosa rose, *Rosa rugosa,* is native in northeast Asia. It is one of the few species having repeat bloom. Typically, the species has single flowers of a light magenta-red color. A white form, *R. rugosa alba,* is also known. The rugose foliage—that is quite disease free—is characteristic of the species. Numerous hybrids have been developed using *R. rugosa* as one of the parents. These hybrids differ greatly in flower size, form, and color. Both the species and the hybrids are remarkably hardy; they deserve to be more widely planted.

Shrub Roses. This is a dumping ground for modern shrub roses developed from hybridization that don't fit into other classes. Many species and cultivars have entered into their development. Hardiness ranges from fully hardy to very tender. A few have repeat bloom, but most cultivars bloom only in the spring.

Species Roses are those occurring naturally in the wilds. Some make attractive ornamentals, but most are inferior to selected cultivars.

With nearly three hundred kinds of old-fashioned and shrub roses in our collection, it is not possible to describe each cultivar and species. Information will be given in tabular form. This information represents published descriptions and observations at the arboretum. Some cultivars have been growing for as long as 15 years. Others have been planted more recently This preliminary evaluation is based primarily on their performance in the arboretum. The chart is self-explanatory. The column marked origin gives the date of introduction when this is known. The size is given in feet and shows height x width. The size of flowers is the width in inches. Under type, S = single; SD = semidouble; and D = double. For hardiness, a scale of 1-5 is used: 1 = fully hardy; 2 = slight dieback; 3 = moderate dieback; 4 = severe dieback; and 5 = death of plant. Hardiness ratings vary greatly for the same plant from year to year, and this range is indicated. No winter protection has been used except for a little straw mulch around the base of some of the more tender classes—such as the Hybrid Musks, Hybrid Perpetuals, and the Kordesii Hybrids (listed under shrub roses).

Class and Name	Year of Origin	Size H x W (feet)	Flower Size (inches)	Flower Type	Flower Color	Time of bloom	Fragrance	Hardiness	Remarks
Alba									
Belle Amour		6 x 5	2½-3	SD	salmon pink	June	yes	3-4	
Celestial		4 x 4		SD	clear pink	June	yes		
Chloris		5 x 5	2½	D	light pink	June	yes	1-4	
Felicite Parmentier	1834	5 x 5	2-3	D	pale pink	June	yes	2-5	
Jeanne D'Arc	1818	5 x 4		D	creamy flesh	June	yes	3	
Koenigen von Daenemark	1826	5 x 5	2½	D	carmine pink	June	yes	1-3	
Maiden's Blush	1738	6 x 6	2	D	blush pink	June	yes	2-5	
Madame LeGras de St. Germain	1846	4 x 6	2½	D	white	June	yes	2-5	
Pompom Parfait	1876	5 x 4	2	D	lilac pink	June	yes	2-4	
Bourbon									
Commandant Beurepaire	1874	5 x 4	3-4	D	striped pink	June	yes	1-3	
Coquette des Alpes	1867	3 x 3	1½	D	light pink	repeat	yes	1-4	
Gypsy Boy		5 x 6	2	D	light purple	June	yes	2-4	
Honorine de Brabant		6 x 5	2-3	D	pink	June	yes	2-4	
La Reine Victoria	1872	5 x 4		SD	lilac pink	repeat	yes		
Louise Odier	1851	6 x 5	2½	D	light pink	repeat	yes	3-4	clusters
Madame Ernest Calvat	1888	6 x 5	2½	D	flesh pink	repeat	yes	1-4	
Madame Isaac Periere	1881		3	D	rose pink	June	yes	4-5	
Madame Pierre Oger	1878	2 x 2	2½	D	lilac rose	repeat	yes	2-5	
Souvenir de la Malmaison	1843	5 x 5	3-4	D	flesh pink	June	yes	2-4	
Zepherine Droughin	1868	5 x 4	3	SD	bright pink	repeat	yes	4-5	
Centifolia									
Blanche fleur	1835	5 x 5	2-3	D	creamy white	June	no	2-4	
Bullata	1801	4 x 5	3	D	medium pink	June	yes	2-4	leaves crinkled
De Meaux	1789	3 x 4	1¼	D	pale pink	June	yes	1-4	
Fantin Latour		5 x 4	2-3	D	blush pink	June	yes		
Juno	1847	4 x 4	3	D	blush pink	June	yes	3	
Petite de Hollande		4 x 4	2	D	blush pink	June	yes	1-4	
Prolifera de Redoute		4 x 4	3	D	medium pink	June	yes	2-5	
Rose des Peintres		5 x 5		D	bright pink	June	yes	4	
Tour de Malakoff	1856	4 x 4	2	D	purplish crimson	June	yes	2-4	
Vierge de Clery		5 x 5	2	D	deep pink	June	yes	1-4	
Damask									
Celsiana	1750	3 x 4	2	D	rose pink	June	yes	1-4	
Cesonie		4 x 6	2¼	D	deep pink	June	yes	2-4	
Four Seasons		6 x 5	2¾	SD	deep pink	repeat	yes	3-4	= R. damascens semperflorens
Kazanlik		4 x 6	1½	SD	rose pink	June	yes	1-2	= R. damascena trigintipetala
Leda		5 x 5	1¼	D	blush white	June	no	1-3	
Marie Louise	1813	4 x 6	3	D	mauve pink	June	yes	1-3	
Madame Hardy	1832	5 x 5	2	D	white	June	yes	1-3	
Omar Khayyam		4 x 4	1½	D	blush pink	June		4	
St. Nicholas		3 x 4	1½	SD	rose pink	June			fruits large, red orange
Gallica									
Alain Blanchard	1829	4 x 6	2¼	S	purplish crimson	June		1-4	round, red fruits
Belle des Jardins	1872	4 x 6	1½	D	white striped on red	June	yes	2-4	
Belle Isis		4 x 4	3	D	flesh pink	June			
Camaieux		4 x 3	1½	SD	splashed crimson on pink	June	yes	1-4	
Cardinal de Richelieu		4 x 5	2½	D	velvet purple	June	yes	2-4	
Charles de Mills		5 x 6	1½	D	crimson maroon	June	yes	1-4	
Desiree Parmentier		5 x 6	2¼	D	vivid pink	June	yes	1-4	

Class and Name	Year of Origin	Size H x W (feet)	Flower Size (inches)	Flower Type	Flower Color	Time of bloom	Fra- grance	Hardi- ness	Remarks
Empress Josephine		4 x 3	2¼	SD	purplish rose	June	yes	1-4	
Grandiflora	1906	7 x 9	3	S	deep pink	June	yes	1-2	very good fruits— round, red
Jeannette		5 x 4	2½	D	light red	June	yes	2-5	
Narcisse de Salvand		5 x 6	2½	D	light pink	June	yes	2-4	
Nestor		5 x 5	2½	D	lilac pink	June	yes	2-4	
President de Seze		4 x 6	2½	D	light purple	June	yes	1-2	
Rosa Mundi	1851	4 x 5	2½	D	red stripes on pink	June	yes	1-4	
Rose du Maitre D'ecole		5 x 4	3	D	deep rose	June	yes	1-4	
Tuscany		4 x 4	3	SD	white flecked crimson-maroon	June	yes	1-4	
Tuscany Superb		4 x 6	3	SD	crimson-maroon	June	yes	2-4	
Moss									
Alfred de Dalmas	1855	3 x 4	2½	D	creamy blush	repeat	yes	2-4	
Anni Welter		4 x 6	3½	D	pink	June		4	
Capitaine Basroger	1890	5 x 6	2¼	D	crimson purple	June	yes	3-4	
Capitaine John Ingram	1854	4 x 4	2¼	D	crimson purple	June	yes	3-4	
Chevreul		4 x 6	3	D	pink	June	yes	3-4	
Communis		4 x 6	1½	D	flesh white	repeat	yes	2-4	
Comtesse de Murinais		6 x 5	1½	D	flesh white	June	yes	2-4	
Crested Moss	1827	5 x 5	2	SD	velvet red	June	yes	2-4	
Deuil de Paul Fontaine	1873	4 x 4	1½	D	purplish red	repeat	yes	2-4	
Duchess de Verneuil	1856	4 x 4	3	D	bright pink	June	yes	2-4	
Eugenie Guinoisseau	1864	2 x 3			cerise magenta	repeat		3	
Gabriel Noyelle	1933	6 x 6	3	SD	light pink	repeat	yes		
General Kleber	1856	5 x 6	2	D	pink	June	yes	3-4	
Gloire des Mousseaux	1852	4 x 4	2	D	pink	June	yes	2-4	
Gracilis		5 x 4	3	D	pink	June	yes	3-4	
Henri Martin	1863	5 x 8	1½	D	crimson purple	June	yes	1-4	
Jeanne de Montfort	1851	6 x 5	1½	D	rose pink	June	yes	2-4	
Julie de Mersent		5 x 6	2½	D	pink	June	yes	2-4	
La Neige		5 x 6	2½	D	purple	June	yes	2-4	
Laneii	1845	5 x 4	3	D	rose crimson	June	yes	3-4	
Louis Gimard	1877	5 x 6	2¼	D	lilac cerise	June	yes	2-4	
Madames de la RocheLambert	1851	5 x 4	2½	D	pink	repeat	yes	2-4	
Marquis Bocella		3 x 2	2½	D	pink	repeat	yes	2-4	
Mossman		5 x 6	1¼	SD	pink	June	yes	1-4	
Nuits de Young		5 x 7	1½	D	maroon purple	June	yes	2-3	
Old Red Moss		6 x 6	3	D	crimson	June	yes	3-4	
Quatre Saisons Blanc Mousseau		4 x 4	2½	D	white	June	yes	4	
Robert Leopold		5 x 6	3	D	flesh pink	June	yes	2-4	
Salet	1854	6 x 6	3	D	light pink	June	yes	2-4	
Striped Moss	1888	5 x 4	1¾	SD	striped pink	June	yes	2-4	
Waldtraut Nielsen		5 x 6	3½		pink	June		3-4	
White Bath	1810	5 x 4	2	D	white	June	yes	2-4	
William Lobb	1855	5 x 6	2¼	D	crimson purple	June	yes	3-4	
Rugosa Hybrids									
Agnes	1922	5 x 4	3	D	amber yellow	repeat	yes	1-4	
Amelia Gravereaux		4 x 3	3	SD	lavender pink	repeat	yes	1-4	
Belle Poitevine	1894	4 x 6	3	SD	purplish pink	repeat	yes	1-3	large orange fruits
Blanc Double de Coubert	1892	4 x 6	3	SD	snowy white	repeat	yes	1-3	orange scarlet fruits
Conrad F. Meyer	1899	3 x 3	3½	SD	silvery pink	repeat	yes		
Delicata	1898	4 x 5	2½	SD	lilac pink	repeat	yes	1-2	
Dr. Echener	1931		3	SD	coppery rose	repeat	yes	2-5	
F. J. Grootendorst			1	D	dark pink	repeat		2-4	clustered flowers

Class and Name	Year of Origin	Size H x W (feet)	Flower Size (inches)	Flower Type	Flower Color	Time of bloom	Fra-grance	Hardi-ness	Remarks
Frau Dagmar Hartopp	1914	3 x 4	3¹/₂	S	shell pink	repeat	yes	2-4	tomato red fruits
George Will		5 x 4	3	D	light red	repeat	yes	1-2	round, red fruits
Grootendorst Supreme	1936	4 x 5	1	D	crimson red	repeat	no	2-4	clustered flowers
Hansa	1905	5 x 7	2	SD	reddish violet	repeat	yes	1-2	red fruits
Max Graff	1919	2 x 12	2¹/₄	S	pinkish white	June	no	2-4	ground cover
Mrs. John McNab		5 x 8	2	D	white	repeat	yes	1-3	
Pink Grootendorst	1923	4 x 4	1	D	pink	repeat		2-4	flowers clustered
Rose a Parfume de l'Hay	1901	4 x 6	3	SD	cherry red	repeat	yes	2-4	
Ruskin	1928	4 x 8	1¹/₂	D	red	repeat	yes	1-3	small red fruits
Sarah van Fleet	1926	4 x 4	3	SD	China pink	repeat	yes	2-4	
Schneezwerg	1912	5 x 5	2	SD	white	repeat		1-3	
Sir Thomas Lipton	1900	4 x 5	2	SD	white	repeat		1-3	
Therese Bauer	1963	4 x 6	2¹/₂	SD	pink	repeat	yes	1-2	
Vanguard	1932	4 x 4		D	salmon orange		yes		
Wasagaming	1939	6 x 7	2¹/₂	D	clear rose	repeat	yes	1-2	
Will Alderman	1949	4 x 5	1¹/₂	D	lilac pink	June	yes	1-3	round, red fruits
Hybrid Musk									
Ballerina	1937	4 x 4	1¹/₂	S	pink, white center	repeat	yes	4	flowers clustered
Belinda	1936	4 x 5	1	SD	bright pink	repeat	yes	4-5	flowers clustered
Bishop Darlington	1926	4 x 5	³/₄	SD	flesh pink	repeat	yes	4-5	flowers clustered
Bloomfield Dainty	1924	5 x 5	1¹/₂	S	canary yellow	repeat	yes	4-5	flowers clustered
Bonn	1950	5 x 4	2	SD	orange scarlet	repeat	yes	4	small, red fruits
Buff Beauty		3 x 4	1¹/₂	D	apricot yellow	repeat	yes	4-5	flowers clustered
Danae	1913	3 x 4	1¹/₄	D	buff yellow	repeat		4-5	flowers clustered
Daphne	1912	4 x 5	1	SD	blush pink	repeat	yes	4	flowers clustered
Elmshorn	1951	4 x 4		D	cherry red	repeat		4	flowers clustered
Felicia	1928	5 x 5	1¹/₄	D	silver pink	repeat		4-5	flowers clustered
Francesca	1922		2¹/₂	S	apricot	repeat	yes	4-5	flowers clustered
Grand Master	1954	3 x 3		SD	apricot pink	repeat		4	flowers clustered
Kathleen	1922	3 x 5	2¹/₂	S	blush pink	repeat	yes	4-5	flowers clustered
Nastarana	1879	3 x 2	1¹/₂	SD	white to pink	repeat	yes	4-5	
Pax	1918	3 x 3	3	SD	creamy white	repeat		4-5	flowers clustered
Penelope	1924	3 x 4		SD	salmon pink	repeat	yes	4	flowers clustered
Prosperity	1919	2 x 4		SD	ivory white	repeat	yes	4	flowers clustered
Rosaleen	1933	3 x 3		D	dark red	repeat		4-5	flowers clustered
Thisbe	1918	5 x 6	2	SD	creamy buff	repeat	yes	4	flowers clustered
Vanity	1920	3 x 3	2	S	crimson pink	repeat	yes	4	flowers clustered
Wilhelm	1934	5 x 7	2¹/₄	D	deep red	repeat	yes	4-5	flowers clustered
Will Scarlet	1948	4 x 4	1¹/₂	SD	scarlet	repeat	yes	4-5	flowers clustered
Wind Chimes		4 x 6	1	S	pink, white center	repeat		2-4	flowers clustered
Hybrid Perpetual									
Alice Vena		3 x 3	1¹/₂	D	plum purple	repeat	yes	3-4	
American Beauty	1875	4 x 5	1³/₄	D	smoky carmine	repeat	yes	1-4	
Arrilaga	1929	4 x 4		D	pale pink	repeat	yes		
Baron Girod de l'Ain	1897	3 x 3		D	white edged crimson	repeat	yes	4	
Baroness Rothschild	1868		1¹/₂	D	deep pink	repeat	yes	1-4	
Barrone Prevost	1842	3 x 3	3	D	purplish pink	repeat	yes	1-4	
Black Prince	1866	3 x 4	2¹/₂	D	dark crimson	repeat	yes	2-4	
Captain Hayward	1893	3 x 3		D	light crimson		yes		
Castilian		3 x 4	1¹/₄	SD	pink		yes	2-4	
Duchess of Sutherland	1839	3 x 3	1¹/₂	D	rosy pink	repeat		2-4	
Ferdinand Picard	1921	4 x 4	2	SD	pink splashed crimson	repeat	yes	2-4	
Frau Karl Druschki	1901	4 x 4	3¹/₂	D	white	repeat	yes	3-4	
General Jaqueminot	1853	5 x 4	4	D	clear red	repeat	yes	1-4	
George Arends	1910	3 x 4		D	rose pink	repeat	yes		
Heinrich Munch	1911			D	soft pink	repeat	yes	5	
J. B. Clark		3 x 3			dark pink	repeat		3-4	
Jubilee	1897	3 x 3		D	velvety purple	repeat	yes		

Class and Name	Year of Origin	Size H x W (feet)	Flower Size (inches)	Flower Type	Flower Color	Time of bloom	Fra- grance	Hardi- ness	Remarks
Juliet	1910	2 x 2	2½	D	rosy red	repeat	yes	3-4	
Mabel Morrison	1878	2 x 2	2	SD	flesh white	repeat		1-5	
Magna Charta		3 x 4	2	D	dark pink	repeat	yes	3-4	
Margaret Dickson	1891	4 x 2	2½	D	flesh pink	repeat	yes	3-4	
Marquis Bucella		3 x 3	2	D	pink	repeat	yes		
Marshall P. Wilder		4 x 3	1½	D	dark pink	repeat	yes	1-4	
Merveille de Lyon		4 x 3	3½	D	rose white	repeat	no	3-4	
Madame Victor Verdier		4 x 4	2½	D	red	repeat	yes	3-4	
Mrs. John Laing	1887	5 x 5	3	D	soft pink	repeat	yes	3-4	
Reine des Violettes	1860	4 x 5	3	D	violet red	repeat	yes	1-4	
Roger Lambelin	1890	2 x 2		D	crimson striped white	repeat	yes	4-5	
Senateur Vaisse		3 x 3		D	deep pink	repeat	yes	4	
Symphony	1935	3 x 2	3	D	flesh pink	repeat	yes	4	
Shrub									
Alexander von Humboldt		4 x 4	1½	D	bright red	repeat	no	4-5	Kordesii hybrid
Amy Robsart		6 x 6		SD	clear pink	June		4	R. eglantera
Apple Blossom		3 x 3	1½	D	pink	repeat	yes	3-5	from Canada
Assiniboine		4 x 4	3	SD	red	repeat		1-2	from Canada
Betty Bland		4 x 4	2	SD	pink	June	no	1-3	small, round fruits
Black Boy		6 x 6	1½	D	crimson purple	repeat	yes	1-4	
Blue Boy		6 x 6	3	D	lilac pink	June	yes	1-4	
Chamcock		3 x 5	2½	D	pink	June		2-3	
Coryana		6 x 6	3	S	lavender pink	June		3-4	
Country Music		2 x 3	2	D	rose pink	repeat			from Iowa
Cuthbert Grant		2 x 2	4	D	red	repeat	no		from Canada
Dr. Merkely		4 x 10	2½	D	pink	June		1-2	suckers freely
Dornroschen	1960	3 x 3		D	salmon	repeat	yes	4	clustered flowers
Dortmund	1955	5 x 5	3	S	bright red	repeat	no	4	Kordesii hybrid
Eddie's Crimson		6 x 8	2¾	SD	red	June	yes	4	R. moyesii
Fruhlingsanfang		5 x 5	3½	S	pale yellow	June	yes	2-4	R. spinosissima hybrid
Fruhlingsduft		5 x 6	3¼	D	light yellow	June	yes	1-5	R. spinosissima hybrid
Fruhlingsgold		7 x 7	4	S	pale yellow	June	yes	1-4	R. spinosissima hybrid
Fruhlingsmorgen			5	S	pink	June		1-5	R. spinosissima hybrid
Fruhlingszauber			3	S	pink	June		2-5	
Golden Wings		4 x 4	3	S	yellow	repeat	yes	4	
Haldie		8 x 10	2¼	D	pale pink	repeat	yes	1-2	large, red fruits suckers
Hanson Hedge		6 x 5	2¼	S	pink	June		1	small, red fruits
Illusion		5 x 10	5½	D	rose red	repeat	yes	4	Kordesii hybrid
Karlsruhe		3 x 4	2¾	D	pink	repeat	no	2-4	Kordesii hybrid
Lawrence Johnston		5 x 6		SD	clear yellow	June	yes	4-5	
Lillian Gibson		9 x 10	1½	D	light pink	June	no	1-2	from South Dakota
Mabelle Stearns		4 x 4	1	D	pink	repeat	yes	3-4	
Maigold		3 x 3	3	D	red	June	no	4	
Mannheim		3 x 3	3	D	red	repeat	no	4	
Marguerite Hilling		6 x 6	1¾	SD	light pink	June	yes	2-4	moyesii hybrid
Martin Frobisher		5 x 5	2½	D	light pink	repeat		2-3	Canadian
Metis		5 x 4	2¼	D	pink	June		2-3	Canadian dark red fruits
Morgangruss		2 x 6	3½	D	creamy pink	repeat	yes	3-4	Kordesii hybrib
Music Maker		2 x 3	3	D	pale pink	repeat	yes		from Iowa
Nevada		6 x 4	5	SD	creamy white	June	no	1-4	
Prairie Dawn		6 x 6	2	D	deep pink	repeat	yes	1-3	Canadian
Prairie Wren		6 x 12	2	SD	pale pink	June	yes	1-2	Canadian
Prairie Youth		6 x 8	2½	SD	pale pink	June	yes	1-2	

Class and Name	Year of Origin	Size H x W (feet)	Flower Size (inches)	Flower Type	Flower Color	Time of bloom	Fra- grance	Hardi- ness	Remarks
Raymond Chenault		3 x 6	3	D	rosy red	repeat	yes	4	
Saarbrucken		4 x 4	3	D	dark red	June	no	4-5	
Sangerhausen		3 x 2	3	D	reddish bronze	June	yes	4	
Scharlachglut		6 x 8	3	S	red	June	yes	4	
Sparrieshoop		3 x 3			salmon	repeat	yes	4	
Stadt Rosenheim		3 x 4	2½	D	pink	June		4	
Stanwell Perpetual		4 x 4	2½	SD	blush pink	June	yes	2-4	
Suzanne		5 x 8	1½	D	pale pink	June	yes	1	suckers
Therese Bugnet		6 x 6	2	D	lavender pink	repeat	yes	1-3	
Von Scharnhorst		6 x 4	3	SD	pale yellow	repeat	yes	2-3	
Wandering Wind		4 x 4	3	SD	pink	repeat			from Iowa
Wasagaming		5 x 5	2½	D	lavender pink	June	yes	1-2	Canadian
Weisse aus Sparrieshoop	1962	3 x 5		S	white	repeat		4	
Wildenfelsgelb		5 x 3	2½	S	pale yellow	June	yes	2-4	
Zweibrucken		5 x 5	3	D	deep crimson	repeat	no	3-4	flowers clustered
Species									
Rosa arkansana		4 x 3	1½	S	pale pink	June	yes	1-2	small, red fruits
Rosa blanda		6 x 7	3	S	pink	June	yes	1-2	small, red fruits
Rosa canina (Dog)		4 x 4	1¾	S	pink	June	yes	1-4	red fruits
Rosa foetida 'Austrian Copper'		3 x 2	2	S	copper red	June	yes	1-4	
Rosa foetida 'Persian Yellow'		3 x 2	2	S	yellow	June	yes	1-4	
"Rosa harisonii 'Harrison's Yellow'		3 x 3	2	D	yellow	June	yes	1-2	
Rosa hugonis (Father Hugo's)		5 x 6	2	S	pale yellow	June	yes	1-3	
Rosa laxa		8 x 9	2	S	white	June	no	1	pear-shaped fruits
Rosa macounii		7 x 9	1½	S	pink	June	yes	1-2	small, red fruits
Rosa mollis		8 x 10	1¼	S	pale pink	June	no	1-2	red fruits
Rosa multiflora		4 x 10	1	S	white	June	no	4-5	clustered flowers small, red fruits
Rosa palustris		4 x 5	2	S					
Rosa pendulina		8 x 8	2	S	white	June	no	1-2	small, orange fruits
Rosa pomifera		8 x 6	1½	S	pink	June	no	1-2	large, red fruits
Rosa primula		10 x 10	2	S	pale yellow	June		1-2	
Rosa rubrifolia (Red Leaf)		6 x 8	1½	S	pink	June	yes	1	small, red fruits
Rosa rugosa (Rugosa)		5 x 10	2	S	pink	repeat	yes	1-2	medium, red fruits
Rosa rugosa alba		2 x 3	2	S	white	repeat	yes	1-2	orange fruits
Rosa rugosa 'Magnifica'		5 x 6	1½	D	lavender pink	repeat	yes	1-2	
Rosa sertata (Garland)		5 x 4	2	S	rose purple	June		1-3	
Rosa setigera (Prairie)		5 x 5	2	S	pale pink		no	2-4	
Rosa soulieana		3 x 6	1½	S	white	June		3-4	orange-red fruits
Rosa virginiana		4 x 2		S	pink			3-4	medium, red fruits
Rosa wichuriana		1 x 8	1	S	white			4-5	small, red fruits
Rosa woodsii		2 x 2	1½	S	pink			3	large red fruits

Index